The Ancient Ones

The Ancient Ones

Book Three
The Gossamer Sphere

By Melissa Conway

Chapter One

London, England

Kevin Guzman watched the three alien spaceships enter Earth's atmosphere. They appeared as bright lights in the afternoon sky far to the south of London proper and streaked across the horizon to the north. Once they broke through the upper atmosphere, the brightness of the hulls faded to a dull metallic black. It was difficult from this distance to tell exactly how large they were, but he thought they looked huge, each maybe as big as or bigger than an aircraft carrier. They were all the same shape, rather oblong, but not smooth. There were various protuberances of different shapes and sizes on the hulls. The ships left no contrail behind them; there was no obvious propulsion system as they floated across the skyline.

Once they disappeared from view, Kevin looked around at the faces of the people nearby. They were standing outside the makeshift military command center that had just been blown up by the Guild, so they were already stunned when the ships made their appearance. Now friends and strangers alike looked awed and terrified.

Kevin wasn't sure how to feel. Of them all, he knew most what to expect, because he'd had mental contact with the aliens. Still, there were many things he didn't know, like why he and Caitlin had gotten the impression that the incoming aliens had been subtly trying to warn them of something.

"They're not far away," Kevin said, drawing the eyes of those nearest him, including General Hawthorne, who was ignoring the persistent ringing of his cell. "They're going to wait until we initiate contact."

"How do you know?" the general asked. "I thought you weren't one of them."

"I'm not. We're not. But I've been communicating with them through the gossamer sphere."

Hawthorne looked at Bill and Seamus. "No one mentioned anything about a 'sphere.' Is that what paralyzed me and – and whatever it did to Collins?"

Seamus gave him an enigmatic smile. "I don't know what Bill told you, but I didn't mention a lot of things. Not trying to hide anything, per se, but there's just so much one can expect the average person to accept in one sitting. It's all rather complicated."

"You'll get no argument from me there," Hawthorne replied. He turned back to Kevin. "Where did they go? The ships."

"They're over the North Sea, above Silverpit Crater, the impact site of the sphere."

"Right, right. The impact site," the general muttered as his phone began to ring again. He looked at the display and grimaced. To Kevin, he said, "I've got to talk to the prime minister. Tell me, in a nutshell, what this sphere is."

Kevin wasn't sure he was the right person to ask, but he tried to sum it up.

"You know about the impact site, about the biometal Bill was attempting to retrieve there?"

After the general nodded, Kevin continued. "It wasn't an ordinary asteroid that hit; the biometal sphere was deliberately sent to our solar system millions of years ago. Not by the aliens who are here now, but by an ancient race, I guess they're extinct now, but these new aliens are using their technology. The sphere was designed to sink into its target planet and form a grid far underground that uses the magnetic field as a sort of communication satellite to connect all of colonized space. The sphere caused the Cataclysm when it began to malfunction and tried to tune itself. I guess you know the rest, about how the biometal changed us."

The general blinked as he tried to absorb the implications but skipped right to the important part. "You can talk to them? The aliens?"

"Yes."

"Excellent." He answered his phone and turned away.

The next several hours were a whirlwind of activity. Kevin and the others like him were whisked away on military helicopters and flown due north. During the flight, Kevin met Tainie, his half-sister, and had a brief, awkward conversation with her before they agreed without words to leave it for another time.

The copter descended over a stubby peninsula that the pilot referred to as Flamborough. Kevin looked out the window at what would normally be a quaint coastal village, with its towering chalk cliffs and windswept green fields, but now the roads were choked with vehicles, and every other field had a helicopter parked in it. The village was fast becoming overrun with people rushing to the coast to get a look at the alien ships looming on the horizon, and the sea was peppered with boats of all sizes.

The copter landed and they were met by two of the same sort of armored vehicles he'd seen at the command center. General Hawthorne told Lieutenant Colonel Paxton to set up roadblocks and only let in officials and the media. Paxton rushed off.

Kevin sat between Tara and Caitlin as they were driven to the tip of the peninsula, where a tent city had been constructed. They stopped at a large tent set up about a hundred yards from the edge of the cliff, its camouflage fabric walls flapping in the stiff breeze. Next to the tent were two plain white vans with satellite dishes on top of them.

As General Hawthorne escorted them to the tent, Kevin said, "We didn't have to get this close for me to talk to them, you know."

"Not my call," the general replied, glancing in the direction of the ships, which were dots on the horizon. "But I like having eyes on them, just the same."

The inside of the tent had portable tables covered with equipment, and military technicians occupied a half dozen folding chairs. Lieutenant Colonel Paxton had somehow beaten them to the tent. He and the technicians came to attention when the general entered.

"Are we ready?" General Hawthorne asked.

"Yes, sir," Paxton replied.

The general put a hand on Kevin's shoulder. "Young man...?"

From the expectant expression on the general's face, Kevin realized the ball was in his court. He looked at Caitlin, who smiled reassuringly. Seamus gave him a thumb's up and Zach said, "Pressure's on, bro." Lizbeth socked Zach in the arm and whispered, "Shut *up!*"

Tara moved to Kevin's side and linked her fingers with his, leaning into his body. "Let's do this."

He nodded, aware that one of the techs had a video camera focused on their group. He slipped his free hand into his pocket and curled his fingers

3

around the biometal kernel. Closing his eyes, he took in a breath and let it out slowly, thinking about the gossamer crown, the cairn and the symbol etched on the spaceships – the three spirals that represented the triskele galaxies.

The last two times he'd spoken with the aliens, he'd been asleep. Merging his mind with the gossamer sphere was dangerous, but the dream state had protected and prepared him to make the connection consciously. He'd done so back at the auditorium, when he'd created the force field to block Collins' signal, and he did so now.

Unlike the first time he'd immersed himself in the sphere, in the final moments of the Cataclysm when it had still been receiving and relaying messages, the connection was quiet. No data streaming in and overwhelming him, but there *was* another presence.

"*Hello,*" he sent into the silver void. "*Welcome to Earth.*"

Vaguely, he heard Caitlin tell the general what he said.

"*Kevin Guzman,*" came the reply. "*Your world is beautiful.*"

"*Thank you. My people are frightened, though. You frighten them.*"

"*We are sorry for the necessity. We mean you no harm. Many among the consortium understand fear.*"

There it was again. That hint of warning. The entity seemed to be speaking plainly enough, yet Kevin felt he should read between the lines. 'Many understand' meant that *some didn't*.

He already knew from his previous 'talks' with them that Earth's atmosphere wasn't compatible with any of the races that made up the consortium. The odds that any two planets in the universe had developed the exact same cocktail of elements, gravity strength, and protection from cosmic radiation were, well, astronomical. He also knew that humanity didn't need to worry that the aliens had come here to take their planet from them. There was no metal or gem or any other precious substance here that couldn't be found in abundance in any number of galaxies they had access to.

Caitlin inserted a comment for Kevin's 'ears' only. "*The general tells me Her Majesty the Queen is rather bravely requesting a face-to-face.*"

Kevin rephrased it for the entity, trying to keep his words as formal as possible. "*My people are also curious about you. May we see what you look like?*"

"*The curiosity is mutual. The consortium has not discovered an intelligent race in a very long time. Our scanners have already detected a fascinating biodiversity here. It is like none other. However, the danger of cross-contamination must be assessed before we truly meet.*"

4

"*Agreed. We measure time in terms of one revolution of the planet on its axis. How many revolutions must pass before you know the danger?*"

"*Calculating...my systems tell me four revolutions will be enough. With your permission, I am sending drones out to scan the remainder of the planet now.*"

Kevin thought it seemed like a reasonable request, so he said, "*That is acceptable.*"

He heard Caitlin tell the general about the drones, but before the information could be disseminated to the world, someone on Lieutenant Colonel Paxton's radio shouted in a panic, "Multiple missiles have been ejected from the enemy ships! We are under attack!"

Paxton yelled back, "Negative! They are *not* missiles. Do not engage! Repeat. Do *not* engage!"

Kevin cursed himself for not anticipating the reaction of a very frightened populace. His fear now was that someone, somewhere, would launch an unnecessary counter offensive. The entire world was watching and waiting. Any number of trigger-happy nations armed with long-range missiles could potentially start a war that Earth would be doomed to lose.

He closed his eyes again to concentrate. "*It is possible,*" he sent to the entity as tactfully as he could, "*That some of my people will misinterpret the purpose of the drones and see their launch as a hostile act.*"

"*I do not understand,*" the entity replied. "*They are harmless.*"

"*I know this, but my people are nervous, and fear makes them–*" he stopped. They had been conversing in the alien's language, and for the first time, Kevin was stuck. He wanted to say that fear made people 'distrustful,' but had trouble finding a corresponding word. When he searched for the concept of trust, it was missing from the language. He tried to find a substitute, but discovered 'doubt,' 'truth,' and 'lie' also did not exist.

Now was a very bad time for him to get hung up on translation. It belatedly occurred to him that the aliens spoke mind-to-mind and might not be capable of lying to each other. Although it struck him as odd that of all the races that made up the consortium, none would have taught this particular entity about truth and lies. Kevin was suddenly overwhelmed with the sense that something was very wrong. He'd learned some time ago to trust it, so instead of attempting to explain the concept, he covered himself by sending, "*Fear makes them defensive.*"

"*Change can be disruptive. Not all take pleasure in discovery,*" the entity sent. "*It is hoped that our association will be mutually beneficial.*"

5

Caitlin relayed this to General Hawthorne, who said, "Kevin, don't agree to anything else. Tell it you aren't the leader here."

After the drone snafu, Kevin was fine with that. *"I am a messenger. There are others who will discuss the terms of our association."*

"Understood. Shall we contact you again once the risk has been assessed?"

"Yes."

"It was nice to meet you, Kevin Guzman. Terminating transmission."

Kevin retreated from the gossamer sphere's silver stream with a deep sigh. He met Caitlin's concerned eyes.

"That went well," Zach said. "Apart from almost starting an intergalactic war."

Chapter Two

Flamborough, England

Lizbeth entered the mess tent, which was filled with soldiers for the dinner hour. She and the others were being given exactly one half-hour to eat, after which they were expected to attend yet another briefing with the General. She doubted the food here was any great shakes, but just the smell of whatever they had on offer made her mouth water. She'd scarfed down a protein bar on the helicopter, but that had been hours ago, and she'd been suffering from increasingly intense hunger pangs for some time now.

Two soldiers had been assigned to guard them, and they'd been counseled to stay together as a group at all times. As their guards escorted them up the main aisle between dozens of portable tables, the din in the crowded tent quieted considerably. It seemed as if all eyes followed their progress to the food tables at the back of the tent. Lizbeth loaded her paper plate with rice and topped it with chunks of what she assumed was chicken swimming in a creamy, orangey-colored sauce. It was all she could do not to start scooping the mystery meal into her mouth with her plastic fork while she waited for her companions to get theirs, but she was too self-conscious to give in to the impulse. The soldiers' conversations hadn't started back up; on the contrary: the mess tent was nearly silent now. The newcomers were being studied, and the unwanted attention made Lizbeth want to run and hide.

Once their group had helped themselves to supper, they turned to the assemblage to look for somewhere to sit. A soldier at a nearby table suddenly stood and lifted his tray. He ran a stern gaze over his tablemates, who didn't wait to be told to vacate. When the table was empty, he nodded respectfully in Caitlin's direction. "Ma'am."

"Thank you, Captain," Caitlin said with a smile.

Lizbeth sat with Caitlin and Seamus on one side of her, and Zach and Tainie on the other. Kevin and the new girl, Tara, sat facing them between their two guards, one of whom was the Scottish soldier who'd spoken to Lizbeth in the auditorium.

The others must have been just as ravenous as Lizbeth after the long, eventful day, because they ate with gusto. No one spoke. The soldiers at the other tables began to talk amongst themselves again, but quietly, as if they didn't want to miss it if someone at Lizbeth's table broke the silence.

After about ten minutes, Lizbeth felt a faint tingling sensation that prompted her to lift her head. In her mind, she heard, "*This is Kevin. I'm using the sphere again to boost my signal. Can everyone hear me? Use your name each time you say something, so we know who's talking.*"

Lizbeth waited until the others had responded before sending, "*Lizbeth here.*"

"*Kevin again. I don't think they're going to leave us alone, so I thought this would be a good way to talk privately.*"

On Lizbeth's left, Zach muttered, "What *is* that?"

As an uninitiated descendant of the folk, Zach would be able to feel the power of the gossamer sphere but couldn't hear Kevin like the rest of them. Lizbeth wished she could tell him what was going on but didn't want the guards to know they were 'talking.' Seamus had gone public with who and what they were but hadn't shared all of their abilities. General Hawthorne knew what they were capable of, but Lizbeth wasn't sure how much he'd told his men. The soldiers would be uncomfortable enough knowing the people they were guarding were shapeshifters - how would they feel if they knew about the telepathy?

Lizbeth leaned into Zach to get his attention, then met his eyes before glancing meaningfully towards Kevin. Zach made a sour face and took an aggressive bite out of his dinner roll before looking away.

After a moment, she heard, "*This is Caitlin. I would like to remind everyone to be extremely cautious. We are useful at the moment, but that could change at any time, and now that we have been unmasked, we are in particular danger. Agent Collins was only one Guild member – there are likely thousands more out there, and we have no way of knowing who they are.*"

Tainie snorted out loud and it must have been she who sent, "*Except for the black hats.*"

"*We cannot count on hats or anything else to reveal our enemies. They could be anyone, anywhere.*"

From the formal wording, Lizbeth knew that last comment also came from Caitlin.

"*And frankly, that's just the danger from those on terra firma.*" Lizbeth glanced at the faces around her, trying to determine who had 'spoken.'

"*Sorry, it's Seamus. And my point is: we don't know what the aliens want.*"

"*Tainie here. I thought they were friendly.*"

Everyone turned to Kevin.

"*On the surface, they're exactly what we'd want them to be,*" he sent. "*As soon as they learned of our existence, they shut down the sphere's efforts to tune itself. If they wanted to destroy us, the easiest way would have been through the sphere.*"

"*Tainie again. What do you mean by, "'On the surface?'*'"

Kevin sighed. "*Something's not right. They're this huge consortium of species from thousands of galaxies, yet the common language they speak has no word for "truth" or "lie." The first entity I encountered, back when we first stopped the gossamer sphere, was able to sort of scour my mind. I don't think it learned much, but it wasn't a pleasant experience. Since then, I've communicated with more than one of them, but none have tried to force me like that. Maybe the first one did it because I came out of nowhere and frightened it. I don't know. I am pretty sure everyone I've talked to was from that same race of beings. Telepaths like us.*"

"*Maybe there's no word for lying because a telepathic race wouldn't be able to lie to each other.*"

Lizbeth didn't know who'd sent that, but it was Kevin who responded: "*That's what I thought at first, but like I said, there are a lot of other races in the consortium. They can't all be telepathic, just like Humanity can't be the only liars in the universe.*"

"*Seamus again. Human history, at least, has shown that a conquering race sometimes forbids its new subjects from using their native language. Perhaps the common tongue has been whitewashed to discourage certain behaviors.*"

"*Or maybe,*" Lizbeth sent, "*their technology is what makes them telepathic. You said that they hadn't discovered a new race in a long time.*

What if they've all been communicating telepathically for so long their original languages have been forgotten?"

Caitlin's head jerked around. "Who said that?"

"Me. Lizbeth."

Caitlin nodded. *"That's an astute observation."*

Lizbeth beamed with pleasure at the rare compliment from her grandmother.

Kevin dipped his head in agreement. *"It's possible there's a perfectly good explanation. I'll try to find out who's in charge next time I talk to them."*

"Tread lightly there."

Again, based on the wording, Lizbeth assumed the last comment came from Caitlin. She turned to her grandmother, but at that moment, she noticed their Scottish guard glancing from face to face, brow furrowed.

"What's goin' on here?" he asked.

Zach uttered a short laugh. "Welcome to my world."

"What do ya mean by that?"

Caitlin shot Zach a cautionary look and said, "It's nothing. What is your name, soldier?"

"Lance Corporal Jaime MacWha, Ma'am."

Caitlin smiled and turned to the other soldier with eyebrows raised inquiringly.

"Corporal Andrew Doyle, at your service." Unlike his earnest but awkward compatriot, Corporal Doyle appeared to be in his mid-thirties, and gave off a confident, almost contemptuous vibe. He wasn't bad looking, but there was something about his demeanor that made it easy for Lizbeth to imagine him going out of his way to run over a stray cat. She knew little about English accents, but he sounded 'upper-class' to her. She also didn't know which of their two guards had seniority but had a feeling that even though MacWha's 'Lance Corporal' sounded fancier, it was trumped by Doyle's plain old 'Corporal.'

"I hope you've eaten your fill," Corporal Doyle continued, "because I'm afraid we must get back."

As everyone began gathering their plates and cups, Zach held out an open napkin. "Left-overs for Caw, please."

"Who's Caw?" MacWha asked.

"My pet raven."

It was a simplification to refer to the raven as a pet, but Zach probably didn't want to try to explain all that was Caw.

10

Lizbeth wouldn't have called it warm inside the mess tent, but its fabric walls had been shielding them from the cold breeze off the ocean. She shoved her hands deep into her jacket pockets as they marched through muddied grass to the command tent. Darkness had almost fallen, but exterior lighting had either not been set up yet or wasn't going to be. Like most every other post-Cataclysm commodity, electricity was expensive.

Lieutenant Colonel Paxton met them at the entrance to the command tent. "Oh good, you're here – we've got a situation, but we won't be needing you, you, you or you." He pointed at Lizbeth, Tara, Tainie and Zach. To Corporal Doyle, he said, "Take them to their quarters."

Lizbeth was about to protest, but Zach beat her to it. "Seriously? You won't be needing me? Then send me *home*. To San Francisco. Because I got better things to do than hang around this miserable country *not* helping you."

General Hawthorne appeared from inside the gloomy command tent and put a hand on Paxton's shoulder. "What the Lieutenant Colonel meant to say was that you've been through rather a lot, and since we don't need all of you to help us stamp out this latest fire, some of you should take advantage and get some sleep."

As placating speeches go, Hawthorne's should have been adequate, but the look on Zach's face told Lizbeth his fuse was already lit, and flowery words weren't going to douse the flame. She put a hand on his arm, but he pulled away irritably.

"Well, if that's true, why don't you send them away," Zach lifted his chin towards Caitlin, Seamus and Kevin, "while the rest of us stay here to help?"

Hawthorne made a contrite face. "Sorry 'bout that. I forgot you can read my mind. Although I honestly didn't—"

Zach cut the general off. "*I* can't read minds." He laughed. "I guess you're right. You *don't* need me."

He turned and strode off.

Without missing a beat, Paxton nodded at MacWha, but before the soldier could follow Zach, Seamus raised a hand. "It may interest you to know that despite Zach's apparent low opinion of himself, he's quite proficient in multiple martial art disciplines and was training to be a police officer back in the States. I advise you not to attempt to force him to come with you."

MacWha looked to his superior officers for confirmation, and Paxton said, "Follow but don't engage. When he's ready, let him know where his quarters are."

11

Chapter Three

Flamborough, England

Zach knew his temper tantrum made him look like a spoiled teenager, but he didn't care. He was sick of being an outsider. Sick of being the only one of their group who wasn't full Fae. Caitlin's decree that she wouldn't allow anyone else to risk their life as an initiate was invalid now that the aliens had arrived. Even Kevin, in all his bland naiveté, didn't trust them. Humanity's very existence might just hinge on the strength of its people – and who were stronger than the Fae?

It was bad enough that Caitlin had denied him the chance to unlock his potential, but the new girl, Tara, had let something slip on the helicopter ride that ignited a fierce, angry burn in his gut.

He'd had no idea who Tara was. After the auditorium blew up, she just showed up with Bill Masters and no one had taken the time in all the craziness to introduce her. When the helicopters arrived, Tara was allowed on board while Bill had to make do with ground travel. The copters had been huge, but the general and his men plus all of Caitlin's group wouldn't fit on just one, so they'd been split up. Zach could see that Tara wanted to ride with Kevin, and vice versa, but she was stuck with Zach and Lizbeth.

Lizbeth managed to doze off despite the noise of the rotors that kept Zach from following suit. He didn't remember seeing Tara among the folk on the ship that helped stop the gossamer sphere, but he'd asked her about it anyway, because it seemed more polite than saying, "So who the heck are you?"

She smiled shyly and answered him, but he couldn't hear her. He made a face, pointed to his ear and leaned closer. She raised her voice and said, "I wasn't there. I just became one of you a few days ago, after I met Kevin."

Stunned, he'd stared at her. She made it sound like Kevin was the one who'd initiated her. Without thinking how his response might affect her, he'd practically shouted, "*How*? How did you change?"

She'd recoiled in her seat, clearly shocked and frightened.

From the seat next to him, Lizbeth sat up. "What's wrong?"

Zach's fury prevented him from answering. He could only shake his head in disbelief. It took a couple of minutes to calm down enough to ask Tara more politely, but by then her lips were sealed. She'd turned away from them with her arms crossed and refused to talk at all.

Now, he walked to the edge of the chalk cliff and stared out over the water towards the alien ships. He knew he'd been followed and wasn't surprised when Lance Corporal MacWha came to stand beside him. The cold, unrelenting wind soon numbed his face, so he almost didn't feel it when his nose started to run. He reached into his pocket for the napkin holding the leftovers for Caw. As if on cue, the sleek black bird landed on his shoulder, right on top of the bandaged gunshot wound he'd gotten earlier. It was just a flesh-wound, but it hurt, so he bent forward and tilted his torso so Caw would be forced to walk across his upper back to the other shoulder. Once the bird had done so, Zach gave him a chunk of meat.

"That your pet raven?" MacWha asked.

Zach didn't really feel like making chit chat, so he sent the soldier a sardonic look. "Nah, wild birds land on me all the time."

MacWha shrugged. "How would I know? I'm human."

Zach blew his nose and shoved the used napkin back into his pocket. "So am I, Dude."

"Oh, that's right. I heard you tell General Hawthorne that you were a, what was it? Descendant of something."

"The Fae."

MacWha nodded. "Right. Sure enough me mum knew fairies were real all along. Is that – do ya hafta be a descendant to change?"

Zach let out a scoffing little laugh. "Used to think so. Now I'm not so sure."

As soon as he caught the glint of interest in MacWha's eyes he remembered what the soldier had said to Lizbeth in the auditorium. "Can I really be like you?" When Lizbeth told him he'd be taking a huge chance with his life if he tried, he'd replied, "It'd be worth it."

To stop MacWha from asking any more questions on that particular subject, Zach said, "I guess you're here to take me to my quarters?"

A flash of disappointment crossed his face, but MacWha nodded.

They began to walk back the way Zach had come. Caw stubbornly clung to Zach's shoulder, wings flapping. Zach gave him another hunk of meat, and the bird flew off somewhere to eat it.

The tent designated for the shapeshifters was one of many set up in rows in view of one of the two lighthouses built on the promontory. MacWha pointed out the 'latrine,' which was a line of Porta-Potties that he referred to as portaloos, and apologized for the lack of showering facilities.

"I understand we're in negotiations with some of the local businesses for access to theirs, though," he said. "In the meantime, you'll find wet wipes in the tent."

Zach thanked him and went inside. There were seven cots set up with barely enough room to walk between them. He was kind of surprised the setup was unisex, but this wasn't the States, and he supposed it would be easier to keep an eye on them if they were all together in one place. The three girls were the only occupants at the moment, however.

"Zach!" Lizbeth jumped up from a cot near the back wall of the tent. He was annoyed that she'd chosen to bunk down with Tara on one side and Tainie on the other. If he hadn't stormed off, he might have influenced her to sleep next to him. Then again, maybe not. She was an enigma; he really had no idea how she felt about him. And with the world in jeopardy again, he wasn't likely to find out any time soon.

She stopped in front of him where he stood near the door flap. "You okay?"

"Fine."

She rolled her eyes and stepped closer, tilting her head back. If he didn't know better, he'd swear she was inviting him to kiss her. He was glad he didn't act on it, though, because she said quietly, "I have to tell you something."

He glanced over at Tainie and Tara, who were sitting together on one cot playing a card game.

"What's up?"

"I think I may know how to change you."

Chapter Four

Flamborough, England

Someone was shaking him. Kevin opened bleary eyes and tried to make heads or tails of the unidentifiable mishmash of blurry light and shadow. It took a moment to realize he had a sideways view of the command tent. He must have laid his head down on his folded arms and dozed off.

Upright and groggy now, he saw it was Caitlin who'd shaken him awake.

"You're back. What time is it?" he croaked.

"Past midnight," she replied.

"How'd it go?"

Earlier that day, British Royal Navy jets had performed nonthreatening flybys around the alien ships, discovering that if they deviated too close, their instruments began to malfunction, forcing them to back off. Boats, too, were affected by whatever was causing this anomaly, and several found themselves adrift until the current took them beyond the equipment failure zone. Caitlin and Seamus had been flown via helicopter to an American aircraft carrier maintaining position along with its battle fleet a kilometer from the ships. From the carrier, the plan had been for them to shift into dolphins to reconnoiter the alien ships from below.

"Not well," Caitlin said.

"Too dark?"

"No, visibility was not an issue."

"Force field?" Kevin asked.

"We are not certain what it was. Before nightfall there were birds flying in the ships' airspace, even landing on them, so it is not an impenetrable barrier. The problem Seamus and I encountered was an inability to hold a shift the closer we got to the ships."

"Whoa. What could cause that?"

Caitlin shook her head. "To my knowledge, only iron has that effect."

"The ships wouldn't be *made* of iron, would they?"

A light laugh escaped her. "Even if a good percentage of their composition is iron, it wouldn't have the ability to affect us from a distance."

Kevin stifled a yawn.

"Come on," she said, ruffling his hair. "We'll talk about this in the morning. We can all use some sleep."

On the way to their quarters, Kevin thought about what little had been accomplished while Caitlin and Seamus had been gone. General Hawthorne's role in the crisis seemed to have been reduced to answering the same set of questions over and over again. Same question, different dignitary asking. To say that people the world over were in a frenzy of panic and despair would be an understatement. If the Cataclysm hadn't severely reduced the world's resources, Kevin suspected the twitchier countries would have already acted against the aliens.

At one point, he'd been asked to contact them again, but his call had gone unanswered. He didn't know why, but speculated it was because he and the aliens had agreed to talk again in four days' time and the aliens, at least, had taken that timeframe literally.

The drones were being tracked all over the world. There were over two hundred of them, each about as big as a mid-sized car. They were oblong and flat on the bottom, resembling huge black, legless beetles. As with the main spaceships, they had no obvious propulsion system, but their pace was swift and never altered. They floated along low to the ground or water, seemingly unimpeded by weather. As far as anyone could tell, the drones hadn't taken any physical samples, and the scanning itself wasn't visible to the naked eye, radar or any other system of human measurement.

Thankfully, the drones either weren't equipped to respond to threats, or the aliens chose not to respond to the many attempts to aggravate them. In India, a crowd gathered around one that had been traversing the bank of the Ganga River, shouting and throwing rocks at it. In the US, a drunken group of men in Kentucky shot at one. The men later reported that the bullets never hit the target – instead they'd supposedly disappeared.

Kevin was grateful that the aliens seemed to understand that earth's diversity included people who were 'less informed' than others.

16

Once Corporal Doyle dropped them off at their designated tent, Kevin collapsed onto his cot. He would have passed out immediately if it weren't so cold. As it was, he barely rolled himself in his blankets before losing consciousness.

He woke sometime later. At least, he thought he was awake. It was still dark, and the left half of his face was pressed into an unfamiliar-smelling pillow that rustled when he moved his head, as if the pillow under the fabric case was wrapped in plastic. The wind had calmed down enough so that somewhere in the tent he heard soft snoring.

The reason he doubted his wakefulness was the nebulous form that stood near the end of his cot. It was a diaphanous female human, the same silvery-blue that he associated with the gossamer sphere, but there was something odd about its aspect; he lifted himself up on an elbow and tilted his head to get a better look. The cloth of her gown was pooled in mid-air strangely, as if a 3D image had been taken of a woman lying down that was being projected like a hologram in an upright position. The woman was reaching towards him, and her lips were moving but no sound came out.

He sensed movement elsewhere in the tent and looked around. Caitlin was sitting up, shoulders rigid, face stiff with shock.

"Do you see her?" he asked.

"It's my grandmother," she replied softly.

A chill raced down Kevin's spine. "That's Queen Wyn?"

Wyn of the Grove, one of the first three shapeshifters. Kevin remembered Caitlin telling them about the warring clans, and how Wyn had placed the crown upon her head and merged her mind with the sphere to implore the gods for help. Instead of a solution, it had killed her – thousands of years ago.

What he was looking at appeared to be some kind of hologram, although there was nothing to indicate the source of the image. He didn't know if the technology to produce such an image even existed, but certainly it hadn't back in Wyn's day. So how was it possible that he was seeing her now?

Caitlin threw her blanket aside and stood. "She's wearing the gossamer crown. The only time she ever wore it was…"

"The day she died," Kevin whispered.

Wyn continued to reach out towards him. For the first time, he noticed an air of desolation about her. "What does she want? It looks like she's saying something."

From the back of the tent came Seamus' voice. "The lore says that on her death bed, the queen was raving. Talking nonsense. Aedn and Tadg thought she'd gone mad."

"She wasn't mad," Caitlin said, "but she'd figured out what the sphere was, and sounded unbalanced when she tried to tell them."

"She knew what it was all those centuries ago?" Seamus asked.

Caitlin nodded. "My mother told me what she said – the gist of it anyway. But it wasn't until the twentieth century – with all the advances in science – that her words began to make sense. It's one of the main reasons I entered so many fields of study, so I would understand what she'd been trying to tell us."

Kevin climbed out of his cot, staying well back of the visage. "The sphere must have recorded her. But how? And why? Is she...do you think this is a message?"

He backed away, unsurprised when Wyn's specter followed him.

"If it is, apparently it's for you." Caitlin's voice sounded hollow.

Kevin cleared his suddenly dry throat and reluctantly reached a hand out until his fingertips brushed those of Queen Wyn. He felt a slight tingle, and that was the last thing he remembered until becoming aware of his surroundings again. He was lying down, and Caitlin was sitting on the edge of his cot, holding his hand. Seamus stood next to her, a worried look on his face.

"How are you feeling?" Caitlin asked.

Kevin took an experimental breath. He had a mild headache behind his eyes, but otherwise felt fine. "I'm okay."

She nodded. "Good. I can't tell you how much I wish we had time to hear that message, but we have a bit of a problem."

Kevin sat up and looked around the tent. Someone had lit an electric lamp and hung it from a crossbar on the ceiling. Tainie and Tara sat together on one of the cots, sharing a blanket around their shoulders. Corporal Doyle and another soldier stood guard at the tent entrance.

There was no sign of Lizbeth or Zach.

Chapter Five

Flamborough, England

Lizbeth had known from the story Tara told her that Kevin kept the biometal kernel in his right pants pocket. According to Tara, she and Kevin had been hiding out in a cairn together near her farm in the Irish countryside. Once he'd dozed off it had been easy for Tara to get the kernel from him, since he slept, as she put it, "Like a badger in winter."

When Lizbeth had gently snaked her hand under the covers and into his pocket, she found that Kevin was indeed a heavy sleeper. But it wasn't Kevin she was worried about. Both Caitlin and Seamus were in the tent, and Lizbeth knew from past experience that her grandmother, at least, slept like a cat in any season.

While she'd gotten possession of the kernel, Zach deftly sliced a hole in the back of the tent, since Lance Corporal Jaime MacWha was still on duty at the entrance.

In Lizbeth's opinion, their escape was nothing short of miraculous.

With only the light from a slim flashlight, she and Zach slunk through the tent city. They didn't make the mistake of assuming everyone was asleep and were careful to avoid alerting anyone to their presence. Once they reached the road, they relaxed a bit.

"So Tara told you we needed a *chicken*?" Zach sounded baffled, understandably.

"No, actually, she didn't seem to understand the significance of the chicken. She told me Kevin had gotten a kernel of biometal from her family's old copper mine, but that he'd dropped it when Bill and his goons showed up, and one of her hens ate it. She didn't know that at the time, of course. All she

19

knew was that her hen started acting funny. I guess it had always been aggressive, but it suddenly got worse and started attacking all the other chickens."

"So she ate it? The hen?"

"Yeah. The next day Kevin realizes where the kernel is and goes back to Tara's farm to get it."

"But Tara ate it."

"No, no. The kernel was still in the hen's guts, which Tara had tossed into the scrap pile in the yard. Kevin got it back." She patted her pocket.

"Okay," Zach said, but he still sounded confused. "I just don't understand why *we* need a chicken."

"I'm getting to that part. Remember the lore from Seamus' website? The story called The First Shapeshifters?"

"Uh, sure."

Lizbeth could tell from his tone that he didn't remember, so she filled him in. "The one about the wild boar that lived in the old mine? The vicious boar with blood-red eyes that started acting erratically?"

"Alright."

Lizbeth had hoped he would put two and two together by now, but he clearly hadn't figured it out yet, so she went on. "Then Aedn killed the boar and Queen Wyn served it to her household. Then Tadg the Small takes some men with him to the mine, and when he comes back, some of them got sick and died. They thought at first the boar meat was tainted, but the men who died were the only ones who *hadn't* eaten it. Get it?"

Zach didn't respond right away. Their footsteps crunched on the gravel along the side of the road as they walked, and Lizbeth was about to explain it to him further when he said, "The mine had biometal in it. Is Tara's mine the same one from the story?"

"I don't know. Maybe. Anyway, after Bill's men show up again, Kevin and Tara run away and hide in this really old Cairn in the hillside. Then Tara takes the kernel from Kevin when he falls asleep."

"But it didn't kill her because she ate the chicken."

"Exactly!"

"Huh." After a few more steps, "and Kevin knew this."

Lizbeth let out a frustrated breath but didn't respond.

It took them about half an hour to get to the village of Flamborough. They spent the next two hours walking up and down the dimly lit streets.

Despite being out in the country, the houses they passed didn't look like farms, and none of the outbuildings resembled chicken coops.

"I think we should try again tomorrow night," Lizbeth suggested. She was freezing and her feet were beginning to ache.

"What?" Zach exclaimed. "For all we know, they've already noticed we're gone. I doubt we'll get another chance to get that kernel from dull-boy."

"You need to stop ragging on Kevin, okay?"

"Maybe I would have. Maybe I already sorta started thinking he wasn't so bad. Then Tara comes along and he can't see past his—"

"Hey!"

He lifted his hands. "You know it's true. She's pretty, and the last time we all got together, he didn't get the girl."

"Oh, and you did?"

Zach ignored her. "Kevin knew initiation didn't have to kill me, and he could have, I don't know, mentioned it in passing. Hey, Zach, all you need is a live chicken and a bit of biometal. But he kept it to himself. Caitlin's flunky to the end."

"Quit it," Lizbeth said. "You're being a jerk."

Zach laughed shortly. "*I'm* being a –" he stopped suddenly and spun on his heel to look behind them. He grabbed her arm and attempted to pull her down, but it was too late. A dark figure appeared from the side of the road.

"If it's a chicken ya want, I know just where to find one."

Lizbeth couldn't see the newcomer's face in what little light shone from the nearest streetlights, but Jaime MacWha's Scottish burr was unmistakable.

"You followed us," she said.

"'Course I did. It's my job." He chuckled. "I kept me distance, though, thanks to the warning about yer trainin'."

Lizbeth couldn't see his eyes, but assumed he directed that last bit at Zach.

"Remind me to punch whoever warned you." Zach's voice was ice-cold.

"Nah. I'm damned grateful he did. Dinna want any trouble from ya."

"You here to escort us back?" Lizbeth asked.

"No. See, I stood at the entrance to yer tent and heard bits and pieces of the story the blond was telling ya earlier, but not enough ta catch the big secret, get it?"

21

This time, Lizbeth knew he was talking to her. It was too late for recriminations, but if she and Zach hadn't been practically shouting at each other, MacWha wouldn't have heard the secret now either.

Zach let go of her arm and stepped in front of her. "Are you Guild?"

"What?" MacWha sounded genuinely insulted. "I was *in* that auditorium, remember? Did I look like I was one of them?"

After a brief hesitation, Zach muttered, "No." Then he said, "Are you armed?"

"Of course."

"That's okay. You'll drop your guard."

"Maybe. But you won't find a chicken in time without me."

Chapter Six

Flamborough, England

Zach didn't trust MacWha, or Jaime, as he'd asked them to call him, but he reluctantly conceded the need for his help. At the rate Zach and Lizbeth were going, it'd be daylight before they got the slightest clue where the nearest chicken coop was – and that was only if they happened to be close enough to hear any roosters crowing.

Jaime headed confidently back the way they'd come, walking past the village proper and then turning down a narrow road that Zach and Lizbeth had passed earlier. Up ahead were a few scattered lights.

"Small family farm," Jaime said. "The family refused to leave when Colonel Paxton tried to appropriate the place for the general. I was with him, so I got a good look around. They got dogs."

"What do you mean? Guard dogs?" Zach asked.

"No, they raise them. Irish Wolfhounds. But they'll bark and alert the owners if we're not careful. The chicken coop isn't far from the kennel."

They decided to leave the road and swing widely around to the far side of the property. It was slow going, and the batteries in Lizbeth's little flashlight had died by the time Jaime whispered, "I think we're close."

"How can you tell? It's pitch black out here." After stumbling through a muddy field for the last fifteen minutes or so, Zach's irritation had reached epic proportions.

"I'll find out," Lizbeth said. Zach heard the sound of a zipper being drawn.

"What are you doing?" Jaime asked.

"Shifting into something that can see in the dark."

"Dunno if that's a good idea," Jaime said. "Dogs'll smell ya. Chickens, too."

"She'll be down wind," Zach pointed out.

"Besides," Lizbeth said, "Pretty sure I smell like a human regardless of what I look like. Brr. Here." Zach felt her press something into his side. "Hold my clothes, would you? I don't want them to get damp."

He pulled the warm bundle into his arms, trying not to focus on the fact that she was standing naked next to him in the dark. He didn't hear her leave but knew when she'd gone. From the bundle of clothes, he felt the power emanating from the kernel of biometal.

After a few minutes, Jaime said, "So how did you know your family comes from the Fae?"

"I didn't. Caitlin told me. Although if you were a descendant you would have noticed some pretty weird things during the Cataclysm."

"Like what?"

"If you didn't feel it, you're not Fae."

"Huh. So let me get this straight. I assume we feed the chicken the biometal, and then what? Eat the chicken?"

Zach hesitated before saying, "Yeah, that's right. Eat the chicken, and then maybe you'll change."

"Maybe?" Jaime asked.

"There's no guarantee, but at least this way it won't kill you trying." Zach didn't feel the slightest qualm about misleading him. In actuality, he felt better knowing Jaime *wouldn't* change. He didn't know the guy. Zach may be young and impetuous, but he didn't want to be responsible for turning a shapeshifter loose on the world when he couldn't vouch for his character.

"Why would it kill me trying?"

Zach sighed. Jaime clearly knew nothing about them at all.

"Way back when, initiates would come from far and wide to be given the opportunity to touch the gossamer crown. Maybe one out of a hundred survived and became a shapeshifter."

"Way back...*when*?" Jaime asked.

"Before the Romans invaded Britain. After that, Caitlin was in hiding with the crown."

"And this crown? Made out of the same biometal we're going to feed the chicken?"

"Exactly."

Zach had no idea how long they waited. It felt like an hour but was probably only ten minutes when a bright light suddenly appeared. It was a flood light mounted at the high point of the largest building, streaming out across the yard. A chorus of barking filled the air.

Jaime muttered, "Damn," and started towards the farm, but Zach stopped him.

"Give her a chance. She's got this."

The next few minutes were tense ones, and Zach was just about to concede that they go look for Lizbeth, when he spotted a low, dark shape silhouetted by the flood light moving swiftly towards them. More lights appeared in the windows of a building that he assumed was the farmhouse. He and Jaime squatted down.

Lizbeth had changed into the same shape she'd taken in the auditorium, a small, sleek leopard, but she seemed to be having trouble navigating. Although she was moving quickly, she stopped and started more than once, and appeared to be weaving as she walked, like she was drunk. It wasn't until she'd gotten closer that he saw her dilemma. The chicken in her mouth was most definitely not cooperating. Its wings flapped frantically, slapping her in the face and obstructing her vision. Zach would have found it funny if not for the fact that a door in the farmhouse opened and a man strode out shouting to the dogs to shut up.

Next to him, Jaime pulled his pistol from the holster strapped to his thigh.

"What are you doing?" Zach snapped. "Put that away."

"Not gonna shoot the farmer," Jaime replied steadily as he lifted the gun and aimed. He fired once, almost casually it seemed to Zach, and the floodlight went out.

"Nice shot." Zach didn't bother to hide the admiration in his tone. At police academy, he'd been an adequate shot at best. Even with a rifle and scope, he probably wouldn't have hit that small a target at that distance, not on the first try, anyway.

"Thanks."

With the floodlight gone, Zach lost sight of Lizbeth, but he could hear her coming – or rather, he heard the chicken – squawking something awful.

"How do we shut it up?" he asked.

"No idea," Jaime said. "All I said is I knew where to find one, not what to do with it once we did."

Lizbeth had finally reached them. A low growl came from her throat, and Zach interpreted it to mean, "Take the chicken out of my mouth this instant." He reached out and encountered feathers, but a split second later, the chicken's claws gouged his hand. That gave him an idea. He'd seen somewhere that you could carry a chicken by the feet. Easier said than done, but with a little persistence and a lot of swearing, he managed to get both scaly feet under control.

Lizbeth must have been waiting for the go-ahead, because she opened her mouth as soon as he said, "Okay, I got it."

The bird continued to struggle until Zach tucked both of its legs into one hand and put the other arm around its body to stop its wings from flapping. Miraculously, all struggling and squawking ceased.

"Where's my stuff?" The direction of Lizbeth's voice indicated she was still crouching after coming out of her shift.

"Over here."

She grumbled about her moist clothes as she dressed, and he said, "I could have taken the chicken from you or stood there and held your clothes, which did you prefer?"

"You could have handed them to Jaime."

"Not with the kernel in your pocket. Hurry up. We need to go. The farmer's back and he's got a flashlight."

They began the long trudge back around to the road. That is, until the sound of dogs howling after the scent reached them – then they began to run.

Chapter Seven

Flamborough, England

"I'm sure they just snuck off somewhere to be alone," Kevin said. "I don't know if you noticed, but Zach's got a thing for Lizbeth and I'm pretty sure she reciprocates."

Caitlin shook her head. "That doesn't explain Lance Corporal MacWha's whereabouts. If he followed Zach and Lizbeth, he should have checked in by now. He has a radio, but he didn't answer when they tried to contact him."

Kevin glanced at their guards and lowered his voice. "You think Zach took him out?"

Caitlin's lips tightened. "He wasn't happy earlier, but it's more likely MacWha followed them. He may have turned his radio off so they wouldn't hear it." She nodded towards the back of the tent where a slit had been cut in the fabric.

As Kevin often did when he felt the need for reassurance, he put his hand in his pocket and felt for the kernel of biometal. When he didn't find it, he experienced a moment of panic that changed to dawning comprehension. He turned to Tara, who was sitting across from him. "Did you say anything to Lizbeth about what happened in the cairn?"

Tara's eyes opened wide in such a look of total devastation Kevin was spurred to jump up and walk over to her. He sat beside her, slipping an arm around her waist. "It's okay," he said quietly. "You had no idea. Don't worry about it, alright?"

"I don't understand," she said. "Doesn't Zach know about the biometal?"

27

Kevin didn't know what to say. Tara still didn't realize that the reason she'd survived the change was because of the chicken. Instead of answering, he turned back to Caitlin. "Lizbeth took the kernel."

Caitlin closed her eyes for a moment. "Those fools."

"I think it'll be okay," Kevin started to say, but a disturbance at the tent entrance stopped him.

A familiar voice said, "Just let them know I'm here!"

"William?" Caitlin rose from where she'd been sitting on Kevin's cot.

Corporal Doyle turned. "It's Bill Masters."

"Yes, thank you. Let him in."

Bill burst into the tent and strode towards Caitlin. "Are you alright?"

"I'm fine. What did you think?"

He sighed heavily, as if he'd been holding his breath for hours. "Any number of things, as it happens. There are a lot of rumors flying around."

"We're tired and Zach and Lizbeth have gone missing, but otherwise all is well. Did you bring it?"

Bill and Caitlin were facing each other, standing so close she had to tilt her head back to look up at him. They began a whispered conversation. Kevin rolled his eyes at Tara, who smiled back.

"Is that her…boyfriend? Husband?" Tara asked quietly.

"No, he's –" Kevin hesitated. "It's complicated."

Tara glanced over at them and said, "Doesn't look complicated to me."

He opened his mouth to reply but was suddenly overcome with a prescient feeling unlike any he'd experienced. Instead of the vague but insistent notion that something bad was about to happen, the sensation was intolerable, and he knew exactly why.

"Uh," he said loudly. "I can't wait any longer. Have to tell you Wyn's message *now*."

Chapter Eight

Flamborough, England

"There's no way we can outrun them!" Lizbeth cried.

Not that what they were doing could be considered running. In the near pitch dark, the muddy, uneven ground made it more of a stumbling, lurching brisk walk. She knew from the sound of the dogs' frantic barking that they were gaining fast.

"Can't you change into something?" Jaime shouted.

"Nothing that would stop *them*," she responded. "They're wolfhounds!"

Caitlin's aunt Felicity once told her wolfhounds were bred to pull knights from their horses.

Jaime, who was running ahead of her to the right, suddenly stopped – she ran right into him or she probably wouldn't have noticed in the dark. Over the barking of the approaching dogs, she heard Velcro tearing and knew he'd pulled his pistol.

"Zach!" she called.

"I'm here." She felt him brush up against her and then suddenly she could see him – still holding the chicken. Turning, she also saw the dogs, four of them, lit from behind by the headlights of a truck. They were running full bore towards them. Zach shoved the chicken into her arms and stepped in front of her, muttering, "Come on, bitches. This ain't my first dog fight."

A whistle pierced the air and to Lizbeth's astonishment, the dogs skidded to a stop maybe ten feet away, their panting breath visible in the cold air. The truck stopped behind the dogs and someone got out and walked towards them. The headlights revealed him to be a white-haired old man holding a rifle.

"I recognized you, Jaime MacWha!" The farmer's accent was similar to Jaime's. "Ya think I don't know it's you?"

"I thought you said you came here to requisition the place for the general," Zach said.

Jaime squinted at the farmer. "I did. Never saw the owners, but I've no idea who that is anyway."

Lizbeth shook her head and sighed. She took a few steps toward the farmer. "I, um, know this looks bad, but there's a really good–"

"No excuses!" the farmer snapped peevishly, lifting the rifle. "That's my chicken! You kids think you can come here and play your games with me?"

Lizbeth held her free hand up placatingly. "No games! And we're not–"

"Mr. Winters?" Jaime asked uncertainly.

"Aye, ya little dunderheed."

"Oh, crap," Jaime said quietly. "That's my next-door neighbor growin' up in Scotland. I gave him hell, but…he'd never shoot me." He raised his voice. "I didn't know it was you, sir! This isn't a prank, I swear!"

"I'd let the dogs have at ya if it weren't for your mum and dad. Now gimme the bloody chicken. And don't think I won't tell them whatcha did."

Lizbeth looked at Zach. His eyes told her he was thinking about making a run for it. Like he'd said earlier, after tonight it was unlikely he'd get another chance at becoming a shapeshifter.

To stop him from bolting, she turned to Mr. Winters. "Your dogs are wolfhounds."

"You'll not be getting any prizes for statin' the obvious, Miss," he replied.

"Do you know Felicity O'Connor?"

Zach gave her a strange look and murmured, "Right, because the world's just that small that he'd know Jaime *and* Caitlin's aunt."

But Mr. Winters said, "Of course I do. Everyone in the business does. Those two on the end there are from her kennel. Brother and sister."

Lizbeth took a few tentative steps forward, encouraged. "So you know how special they are."

"The dogs? What's that got to do with the chicken ya stole?"

"Because they're special," she said, tilting her head and giving him a meaningful look. According to Felicity, whose family had been breeding them for centuries, wolfhounds were descended from the Cù Sìth, a giant, supernatural, red-eyed dog from the Scottish Highlands. Felicity's dogs in particular had a very unique ability to find things.

"Are you daft, girl?"

"No." She sighed. He either didn't understand her or was very convincingly pretending not to. She handed the chicken back to Zach and took her jacket off, shivering when the cold air hit skin sweaty from her run. She handed the jacket to Zach, who said, "What are you doing?"

She didn't respond, instead asking Mr. Winters, "Have you heard on the news about the shapeshifters?"

"Aye. You've taken the chicken for the fair folk then?" he scoffed.

"Yes." Lizbeth said. "Because I'm one of them."

Mr. Winters looked at Jaime, who said, "It's true."

The old man blinked several times. "Well, Jaime MacWha, I've known you to be a lot of things, but a liar weren't one of 'em."

"They're here because of the aliens offshore," Jaime said. "I'm not lyin'."

Mr. Winters frowned. "Prove it."

Lizbeth didn't ditch her clothes this time, just shifted silently into the black leopard. Unable to maintain her upright position, she dropped to all fours, keeping a close watch on Mr. Winters' face the entire time. The dogs began to whine as the old man's mouth dropped open. With Lizbeth's enhanced vision, she was able to see tears start in his eyes.

"Saints preserve us," he murmured. "It is true."

Lizbeth shifted back and got to her feet, adjusting her clothes. "We need your help."

Mr. Winters nodded and kept nodding as he said, "Alright. But yer payin' fer that bird. These days a good layin' hen like her is worth her weight in gold."

Lizbeth took her jacket from Zach and shrugged into it. "I don't suppose you have any eating hens, then?"

"I've a few older birds that aren't laying as much. Unless…you think my hens are special, too?"

She wasn't sure if he was serious or joking, but she replied, "No, the chickens aren't special."

Mr. Winters' lips twisted, and he waved for them to follow him. As she and the others got into the truck, she caught him staring and took the opportunity to reach out with her gossamers. As she'd suspected, he knew more than he was letting on.

Chapter Nine

Flamborough, England

Mr. Winters stopped the truck near the chicken coop and asked, "What do you need me to do?"

Zach didn't want Jaime blabbing what they were really up to, so he answered quickly, "We need to feed the hen something before we, uh…" he looked down at the bird resting quietly in his arms. This wasn't the first time he'd felt a pang at being a carnivore, but it was the first time he'd been so close to his meal before it became one.

"I get yer meanin'," Mr. Winters said. "What is it ya want to feed it?"

"It's something a chicken wouldn't normally eat," Lizbeth said. "A kernel of, uh, metal."

"Chooks routinely eat stones to aid in digestion," Mr. Winters replied, "but it's the middle of the night, and they're all roosting. Here, give me that one. I'll get a different bird."

Zach handed the hen over with little fuss. When Mr. Winters had gone, he said, "I hope we can trust him."

In the passenger seat, Jaime's shoulders rose and fell. "He's an odd old sod, but what choice do we have?"

Zach looked out the window at the blackness. Morning was still several hours away. From outside the truck, he heard the clucking of several chickens. Less than a minute later, Mr. Winters was back.

"Well, get out then," he said. "Unless you want to do this in the lorry?"

They all trooped out and followed the old man into the barn. The truck hadn't been running long enough to get warm, and the barn felt toasty in comparison. Mr. Winters lit a kerosene lamp, grousing a bit about the cost of fuel.

"Alright then, hand it over," he said. "Force-feeding a chicken's not a doddle."

"You can't touch it," Lizbeth said. "It'll kill you."

Mr. Winters' head pulled back on his wrinkled neck. "Put that in the 'failed to mention' category and mark it important. If you're looking to kill the hen, there's faster ways to go about it."

"Can we just do this together?" Lizbeth asked. She sounded bone weary to Zach and he felt a twinge of guilt. She was doing this for him, totally disregarding the inevitable fallout from Caitlin.

"Sure and we can try," Mr. Winters said.

It took them about ten minutes to get the hen to swallow the biometal kernel. Afterward, Mr. Winters put the bird in a wire cage. "I suppose you'll be needin' to keep an eye on her, so why don't we move this party to the house?"

It was a short walk to the main farmhouse. A red-haired woman in a lavender housecoat met them at the door. She appeared to be younger than Mr. Winters by at least a decade, but by the quick hug they exchanged, it was clear she was his wife.

"Ha," she said, pointing at Jaime. "I was right. It *was* you. Thought I saw you earlier when they came to take our home from us."

"Hello Bess," Jaime said. "How are you?"

"A bit gutted by everything that's happened, but otherwise brill. Your mum said you'd joined the army. I don't suppose you can tell us what the aliens want?"

"I can't," Jaime replied, "but only because I've no idea."

Bess turned shrewdly narrowed eyes on Zach and Lizbeth. "And who are your friends?"

"They need our help," Mr. Winters said. "That's all ya need to know."

His wife's left eyebrow rose as her gaze dropped to the chicken in the cage.

Mr. Winters heaved a sigh and conceded, "It's not my story to tell."

Bess invited them all into the kitchen, where she put a pot on to boil and bustled around fixing them a snack while Lizbeth told her what she'd told Mr. Winters. Bess paused with her hand outstretched towards the steaming teapot when Lizbeth admitted to being a shapeshifter. It was only a brief hesitation, but Zach suspected the news was a deep shock. He'd noticed in the

34

entryway a portrait of the Virgin Mary on the wall and wondered how her faith had been affected by the aliens' arrival. Whatever her thoughts on the subject, Bess kept them to herself, pouring the tea as if members of the "fair folk," as Mr. Winters had called them, sat at her table all the time.

"So you fed the chook this kernel," she said, hand on the back of her husband's chair. "I assume it's magical? Is the hen going to change into something else?"

Zach couldn't help himself – he laughed.

Bess pursed her lips and glared down at him. "I, for one, don't find any of this amusing."

"I'm sorry," Zach said, still fighting a smile.

"Ignore him, he thinks everything's funny," Lizbeth said. "The kernel isn't magic. Everything that's happened has been…scientific in nature. It will alter the chicken's makeup on a molecular level."

Since Lizbeth had only figured out how to change him a few hours ago, Zach was impressed with her answer.

"And then what?" Bess asked.

"Uh, then, well, Zach and Jaime are going to, um, eat it. The – the chicken." Lizbeth sounded less sure of herself now. She glanced over at the bird in its cage and then frowned down at the table.

"Ah," Bess said. "And afterward? What happens to those who eat the chicken?"

Jaime answered before Zach could stop him. "*They* change. If they're lucky."

Bess stared at him as all the color leached out of her face. Mr. Winters leapt up out of his chair, put an arm around her shoulders and sat her down. "It's alright, mama, it's alright."

He looked at Lizbeth, face hard. "We'll help you, but you can be sure we won't be sitting down to that meal with you."

Zach didn't know what motivated the man to sound so adamant, but he didn't get a chance to ask.

The chicken began to beat its wings against the walls of its cage.

Chapter Ten

Flamborough, England

After Kevin's announcement, he found it hard not to immediately launch into further speech, but Bill asked incredulously, "Message from *whom*?"

"My grandmother," Caitlin replied.

"But she's—"

"Yes, dead for centuries. Hush now. Can't you see Kevin must speak?"

Kevin was still sitting next to Tara, so tense he felt as if every muscle in his body was clenched, every tendon stretched to its limit. Images and concepts were rapidly unfolding in his mind. It was a struggle to find a beginning point; a way to disseminate the message so it made sense to those listening.

"The message wasn't actually from Wyn," he said. "It came *through* her from…they were the Ir. The oldest race in the known universe. They were…a metallic people, composed of the iridium biometal, only—only not. They were changed before they were vanquished by a race called the…um, I don't know what to call them. The word in my mind translates to 'omnipresent.'"

"You mean like God?" Seamus asked.

"That's pretty much how they saw themselves, yes. They were a highly advanced technological society that emerged from the triple galaxy. I guess they felt their evolution was at a standstill and were compelled to search for ways to bolster and enhance it. They traveled the star systems, finding unique raw biological specimens for their…experimentation is the closest word I can find, but for them it was more like a compulsion. Their society was based on not just solving problems but finding problems in order to solve them. The more unique and difficult the challenge, the more status for those who solved it. Whenever they found a sentient race, they..."

He paused as examples of what they had done spooled horribly through his mind.

"Attacked?" Bill asked.

"No. No, they never attacked anyone. Didn't want or need to. Their specialty was passive aggression. Win them over by offering something they needed and then find a use for them and...control them."

"How?" Seamus had moved to stand next to Caitlin.

"Through communication," Kevin said. "Offer them something they couldn't refuse, usually something that would significantly enhance their lives or save them from self-destruction. I guess the fear of global annihilation is pretty universal. But in order to get it, they had to agree to allow them to...study them."

"I assume 'study' is a euphemism?" It was Seamus, prompting him again. Kevin knew there were long pauses in his narrative, but he couldn't help it. It was difficult to condense everything in his mind into a cohesive story.

He nodded. "They had to keep up appearances. They were the benevolent saviors, but secretly committing atrocities. The denizens of each world they encountered had different chemical and physical makeups, so sometimes it took," he blinked as he tried and failed to compensate for the time concepts, "a long time."

"You said they controlled them through communication," Caitlin said. "I don't understand that."

"Sorry. Their technology allowed them to communicate mind-to-mind. Their experimentation was largely focused on giving these other races the same...benefit. But the real goal was to bring them into the fold."

"Mind control?" Seamus asked.

"More like eavesdropping. No one was ever...alone. Not even in their own mind."

"Like what we were talkin' about in the mess tent," Tara said. She'd been holding Kevin's hand, and he gave hers a gentle squeeze to acknowledge her comment.

"What happened when the Omnipresent found the Ir?" Caitlin asked.

"They were ecstatic. The Ir were shapeshifters and natural telepaths."

Caitlin tilted her head, eyeing him warily. "Like us."

"Yes, although technically, they were one huge organism that could split into many and then join back up again. And the shapes they could take were unlimited. Not like us. They had once been a star-faring race themselves, able to communicate with each other across the vast emptiness of space. To the Omnipresent, the Ir were…"

"Irresistible?" Seamus asked, twisting his lips at the pun.

"More so than any race they'd ever come across," Kevin said. "But the Ir wanted nothing to do with them."

"I take it that didn't stop the Omnipresent," Bill said.

"No," Kevin replied. "It didn't."

"What happened?" Tara asked.

He hung his head to hide the look in his eyes but couldn't keep the thickness out of his voice. "They went to war, but the Omnipresent couldn't win because the Ir couldn't be killed. Even capturing one was almost impossible."

"Almost?" Caitlin said.

"The Omnipresent did what they did best. They experimented. Found a way to control the Ir and…make use of them."

He felt a hand on his shoulder and looked up into Caitlin's concerned face. "Tell us."

He blinked and the tears he'd been holding back spilled over. "The Gossamer Sphere *is* the Ir."

Chapter Eleven

Flamborough, England

Lizbeth woke to the smell of coffee and roasted chicken. She was lying on her side on the Winters' blue settee; across from her on the matching sofa, Jaime was just beginning to stir.

"Up and at 'em, then," Bess' voice came from the kitchen entryway. "Breakfast is ready."

Lizbeth suppressed a groan of protest as she sat up and glanced at the clock on the mantel. She'd gotten less than two hours sleep – just a nap, really. They'd stayed up until the wee hours preparing this very meal. She placed her hand over her pocket, sensing the biometal kernel she'd recovered from the doomed chicken's entrails. 'Breakfast' smelled wonderful, but the memory of the evening's work soured her stomach. Good thing she didn't have to eat any of it.

In the kitchen, Zach was seated at the table, hands curved around a mug of coffee. It was clear from the dull look in his eyes that he'd accomplished his intention of staying up all night. He'd pulled Lizbeth aside just before she'd curled up on the settee to tell her he didn't trust Mr. and Mrs. Winters.

"They're helping us, but I can tell they don't want to. I'm going to stay up and keep an eye on the oven."

Mr. Winters was nowhere to be seen, and Bess seemed out-of-sorts. She dropped a couple of hot pads in the center of the table and shoved her hands into quilted mitts before taking the roasting pan out of the oven. She set it on top of the hot pads and then put her mitted hands on her hips.

"I trust you'll find my cooking adequate. After you're done, we'd be much obliged if you would take the leftovers and leave."

Before the first three words left her mouth, Zach had grabbed the carving knife and begun slicing. Lizbeth smiled at Bess and murmured, "Thank you." She hadn't had the opportunity the night before, but since Bess was staring at her, Lizbeth reached out with her gossamers and touched her mind. The older woman was indeed severely irritated. Jaime pulled a chair out for himself, and just before Bess' eyes broke contact with hers, Lizbeth got a flash of just what it was she was so upset about.

As it happened, Jaime brought the subject up. "How's Emily?"

"You don't know?" Bess asked.

Lizbeth would have kicked Jaime under the table, but it was too late. He was busy following Zach's example and had taken a slice of steaming hot chicken breast between his fingers. He blew on it and asked absently, "Know what?"

Bess remained silent until Jaime looked up at her. The weak morning light shining through the window over the sink lent her face a haggard bent. Jaime didn't strike Lizbeth as particularly astute, but even he recognized grief when he saw it.

He forgot all about the chicken as his forearm slowly lowered to the table. "Aw, no. Not her."

Bess' chin quivered. "She was in New Zealand on holiday."

New Zealand, situated along the active tectonic region known as the Pacific Ring of Fire. The Cataclysm destroyed entire cities, and in some cases almost wiped out whole countries, New Zealand among them. Millions of people had perished, many more were displaced.

Lizbeth opened her mouth but closed it again as Bess hastily left the room. After a moment Lizbeth gestured towards the chicken. "Now we know why she and Mr. Winters want nothing to do with that."

"Why's that?" Jaime asked.

"Because they lost…I assume Emily was their daughter?" At Jaime's nod, she continued. "What's the point of living forever if you have nothing to live for?"

Zach had stuffed his mouth full of chicken, but he spoke past it. "The Fae don't live forever, though. Lot of ways to die."

"But they've got several advantages to prevent it." Jaime took a big bite of chicken and grinned. "*We've* got, that is."

"No guarantees," Zach reminded him.

"Yeah, I know. How much do we have to eat?"

Lizbeth recalled what Tara had told her: that her illness had killed her appetite and she'd hardly eaten any. "Not much. Maybe we should go."

"Good idea," Mr. Winters said from behind her. "My wife has gone to bed. I'll find you a container for the leftovers."

Chapter Twelve

Flamborough, England

On the walk back to the tent city, Zach had a hard time keeping his elation under control. He wanted to shout and pump his fists into the air in victory, but Lizbeth was subdued above and beyond what lack of sleep should have done to her. She had to be dreading the confrontation with Caitlin. Which reminded him: as soon as they got back, Caitlin would confiscate the kernel and ensure it was put somewhere safe. It was now or never.

He took Lizbeth's hand and stopped her, glancing over at Jaime. "Hey man, could you give us a sec?"

Jaime shrugged and walked ahead. As soon as he was out of earshot, Zach said, "Give it to me."

"What?! It's too soon. You haven't even digested your food yet. Tara didn't touch the kernel until the next day."

Zach bit the inside of his lip. The last thing he wanted was to invalidate everything they'd accomplished by acting too soon. That, and if she was right, touching the kernel now would likely kill him. Before he could decide what to do, however, Jaime called out, "Heads up."

An army truck was coming rapidly up the road.

"What do you want to bet that's for us?" Lizbeth asked.

"Let me have it."

"No!"

"Lizbeth, it's my last chance and you know it."

She yanked her hand free from his and stepped back. "I won't let you die."

"What the hell are you talking about?" Jaime had walked closer without them noticing. "Who's going to kill him?"

"He's *going* to kill himself," Lizbeth said through gritted teeth.

"You don't know that." Zach grasped her shoulders and pulled her stiff and resisting body closer before resting his forehead on her shoulder. "*Please*," he whispered intensely.

The truck pulled up next to them and stopped. Caitlin was the first one out, and she looked furious. She went straight for Lizbeth. "Hand it over."

Lizbeth shook her head. "No. Just let us have it for a couple more hours."

"Why?" Caitlin asked.

Zach held up the paper grocery sack with the leftovers inside. "Because of this."

"And that is...?" Kevin had come to stand next to Caitlin. "Let me guess: chicken."

Caitlin looked at Kevin as if he'd said, "Pterodactyl."

Kevin reached for the paper sack, but Zach jerked it out of reach, so Kevin dropped his hand and turned to Caitlin. "I was going to mention this in the tent. Tara told Lizbeth what happened to her, and Lizbeth put two and two together. The chicken's tainted." He looked at Lizbeth. "Right?"

Lizbeth pressed her lips together and stared Kevin down. "You could have told him."

"I would have," he replied, looking back and forth between Lizbeth and Zach. "Just didn't have a chance." He gestured to the sack. "How much is left?"

Zach shrugged. "What difference does it make?"

Kevin directed his gaze toward the ocean and the alien ships that hovered on the horizon. "Because things have changed, and we need all the help we can get."

43

Chapter Thirteen

Flamborough, England

"So you think the aliens out there are the Omnipresent?" General Hawthorne asked.

They were in the command tent sitting and standing around the 'conference table,' which was the exact same kind of portable table as the ones in the mess tent. Kevin had just brought the general and his officers up to speed. Caitlin, Seamus and the others were all there – and Kevin had insisted Jaime be included, as well. The paper sack of leftover chicken sat conspicuously in the center of the table.

"It's been well over 65 million years if you estimate the time it took the gossamer sphere to reach earth," Kevin replied. "At this point, it's hard to say who they are exactly, but the message from the Ir was triggered by their arrival, and they can talk to me telepathically, so at the very least they've inherited Omnipresent technology."

The general shifted in his seat, a deep crease between his eyebrows. "Pretty compelling evidence. Best we assume the worst."

"I don't get it," Colonel Paxton said. "How did the Ir manage to leave the message if they were all killed?"

Kevin rested his elbows on the table and rubbed his chin wearily. "The war went on for a long time because the Ir were very hard to kill. They could literally sort of melt through solid objects, which made them hard to catch. The only thing that killed them was prolonged contact with iron – not that killing them outright was the Omnipresent goal. The Ir were unique, and in the Omnipresent eyes, irreplaceable. But they recognized the very real

44

possibility that the Ir might win the war, so they changed their game plan. Once they figured out how to sort of reverse-bioengineer the Ir molecular structure, creating the biometal, it was game over."

"Essentially?" Seamus asked. "Because the biometal *is* a living thing, right?"

Kevin nodded, recalling how Caitlin had once described it as rudimentarily alive. "They needed the Ir alive but not…sentient…in order to use them."

"None of that answers my question," Colonel Paxton pointed out.

"I'm getting there," Kevin responded. "Once word reached the Ir that the Omnipresent were going to wipe them out and use their collective corpse as the infrastructure for their new communication system, Ir rebels…embedded the message, the truth about what happened to them, in what we would call their DNA."

"You said the Ir were shapeshifters and telepaths, like you," Hawthorne said. "Can't be a coincidence."

Kevin shook his head. "It's not. Caitlin postulated some time ago that the gossamer sphere hit our planet by accident. She was both right and wrong. Once the Omnipresent neutralized the Ir, they began targeting planets with strong magnetic fields so they could harness that energy and use it for their new multi-galactic communication network. Apparently, they were careful to avoid planets that could potentially support life. A band of Ir survivors managed to infiltrate the launch station and change the trajectory on some of the spheres before they were caught. One of those spheres came to earth."

"Why'd the Omnipresent avoid planets that could support life?" Zach asked. "Sounds like they weren't all that concerned with preserving it."

"Uh, well, they were, actually, as long as that life was under their control," Kevin said.

"So the Ir sent the gossamer sphere to earth knowing it would wipe out the ecosystem?" Zach made an exaggeratedly confused face.

"They were desperate. They chose a planet far from the beaten path in the hopes that eventually they would be…resurrected."

"Is that possible?" Bill exclaimed.

The corner of Kevin's mouth crooked upward. "Kind of."

"When the sphere hit earth," Caitlin said, "all surviving creatures were exposed to the biometal and their genetic blueprint was altered. We are not the Ir, but we *are* their legacy. And now we know their story."

45

Hawthorne sighed. "Assuming the aliens out there are the descendants of the Omnipresent, we can expect them to treat us the same way they treated every other species they encountered. Any thoughts on how to prevent that?"

"We don't have a plan yet, other than to bolster our numbers," Kevin said.

"And that means...?" The intensity in Bill's eyes told Kevin he knew exactly what it meant.

Caitlin, gaze fixed on the surface of the table, answered in a gentle, controlled voice. "Given the obvious advantages we, the Fae, have over normal people, we think it prudent that a task force be established, and that the members be initiated as Fae. In the past, that meant only one in a hundred would survive, but we've recently discovered how to change them without any apparent risk. Those chosen would need to have certain qualifications, of course."

The breath left Bill's lungs in a wordless, half questioning, half joyful sound. Caitlin looked up at him, a hint of a smile on her lips.

"I'm not sure that's warranted," Hawthorne said. "The aliens can read Fae minds. If they do turn out to be hostile, it could prove detrimental."

"Hostile or not, they are our technological superiors," Caitlin replied. "We can assume they have accessed our internet and tapped into our communication systems, likely at the highest levels. At the end of this four-day 'assessment period' they will have studied our history and know exactly what our defense capabilities are. We will lose any conflict with them, and if the message Kevin received is still at all relevant, they will eventually develop the ability to read – and control – human minds anyway. For all we know, that's already in the works, especially given the fact that humans are to all intents and purposes descended from the Ir. I suggest we don't make the mistake of thinking they don't know exactly what we are."

Hawthorne's head twitched to one side in a minutely negative gesture. "I wouldn't dream of it. In fact, if their goal *is* to offer us something we can't refuse in exchange for controlling us, there's a good chance they already know more about us than we do. If a conflict does arise, and we're to have any chance against them, we must come up with a viable defense. And I don't think I'm exaggerating when I say the fate of mankind rests on our discretion. Do you all understand?"

His stern gaze swept the occupants as everyone nodded or murmured assent.

"Right then," he continued. "What qualifications should we look for?"

"The usual," Caitlin said. "Intelligence, willingness to take risks and follow orders. They must also understand that Fae couples cannot have children together, and children between Fae and human rarely survive. I would like to interview the candidates personally."

Kevin knew this meant she would ask them questions and read their minds to determine their integrity.

"We'll start with present company," Hawthorne said. "Of those not already Fae, who would like to volunteer?"

Every hand shot into the air.

Chapter Fourteen

Flamborough, England

Lizbeth hadn't ridden a bicycle since her elementary school days in New Orleans. The one she was riding now had a hard seat and squealed like an angry pig whenever she applied the hand brakes. She didn't know where the army had gotten the rag-tag selection of non-motorized vehicles that had been made available for their use, but she suspected her ride, at least, had come from a junkyard or someone's old barn. At least her bike was made for adults; both Tainie and Tara were seated on children's bikes – Tara's even had perky pink tassels hanging from the handlebars. Kevin was riding an old ten-speed, but Zach and Jaime were on mountain bikes, and Zach, at least, was in his element if the constant wheelies and bunny hops were any indication.

They were on their way back from a hotel in the village that had been abandoned like so many other places of business after the Cataclysm. General Hawthorne had sent a crew in to secure the location and fire up the water heaters. It was the third day since their arrival, and Lizbeth had very much enjoyed her shower, even if it was short and the water wasn't exactly hot.

Project 'Welcoming Committee' was well under way. Both Zach and Jaime had been exposed to the biometal, touching not Kevin's kernel, but the gossamer crown itself, which Bill had recovered from its hiding place and brought with him at Caitlin's behest. Neither Zach nor Jaime had gotten sick, although the whites of Jaime's eyes had gone red. Zach's mood swung between ebullience and impatience.

"What if my shapeshifting doesn't kick in in time?" he'd asked earlier that day.

"In time for what?" Lizbeth had responded.

"Our alien overlords making their move. What else? We've only got one more day of radio silence."

"To be honest, I don't think we stand much of a chance if they do."

Zach snorted. "Ye of little faith."

Privately, Lizbeth thought his innate self-confidence had crossed over into cockiness, but she was glad he'd finally gotten his wish. He was Fae.

She'd taken up the rear of their little bicycle convoy, and nearly failed to notice that everyone had slowed significantly. She squeezed hard on her brakes, wincing at the resulting squeal. As she came to a juddering halt a few inches from Tara's back tire, she glanced up and saw why they'd stopped.

One of the alien drones was cruising through the field to their left, about two feet above the ground. If it didn't change course, its path would take it across the road and through the center of the Army's tent city.

"Let's go!" Zach waved an arm before peddling rapidly down the road, clearly planning to intercept it. He underestimated the speed of the drone, however, missing it by several seconds. He and Jaime didn't hesitate to chase after it, but the rest of them followed more cautiously.

Lizbeth peddled as fast as she could, but her bike couldn't keep up the pace, and she fell behind once more. When she reached the place in the road where the drone had crossed, the hair on the back of her neck lifted in a visceral response to...what? It felt very much as if she was in the presence of the gossamer crown, but there was nothing there – nothing but the invisible trail of the drone.

She finally caught up to the others, but only because they'd stopped again and were staring open-mouthed at the drone, which hovered now in place outside the command tent. In the three days since the aliens had been scanning the earth, to her knowledge none of the drones had so much as slowed down.

Excited voices echoed throughout the camp, but Lizbeth found she couldn't look away from the drone. It seemed to be emitting a strange vibration that felt as if a cat were purring soundlessly inside her skull. A low, cylindrical protrusion on the front of it twisted open like the aperture on a giant camera. She took a step back as a fear unlike anything she'd ever experienced swept over her.

General Hawthorne hurried out of the command tent with Caitlin, Seamus, and Colonel Paxton, stopping short when he caught sight of the drone.

"Nobody move!" he said. "Do nothing to aggravate it."

In what seemed to be in direct opposition to the general's order, Kevin took an awkward step towards the drone. Lizbeth turned incredulous eyes on him as he took another, his right foot scuffing through the dirt as if he were trying to stop himself.

"I said freeze, Mr. Guzman!" Hawthorne snapped.

"I can't help it!" Kevin gestured downward as he took another unwilling step. His hips were thrust forward oddly, while his upper body leaned back away from the drone. "It's pulling the kernel!"

Zach leaped to his aid, grasping his upper arm. Jaime joined him on the other side, but they were unable to stop Kevin's inexorable forward progress.

Afraid the drone would suck Kevin into its maw, Lizbeth cried, "Take his pants off!"

"I can't!" Zach had wrapped his arms around Kevin's chest, his face red with effort.

Lizbeth ran to help, ignoring her embarrassment to rapidly unbutton Kevin's jeans. The white cotton inner pocket flipped out of Kevin's open fly, and with a tearing sound, the kernel ripped through the material and shot into the drone. Kevin, Zach and Jaime sprawled backward into the dirt. The aperture closed and the drone turned from its path towards the sea.

Those present watched in stunned silence as it headed on a direct course to the alien ships.

Zach scrambled to his feet. "Are we just going to let it take it?"

Caitlin shook her head. "What else can we do?"

"We can go after it!" Zach's gaze skimmed the faces around him, looking for support.

"To what purpose?" Caitlin asked.

He threw his arms into the air. "It's better than just sitting around waiting for whatever's next!" He broke into a run after the drone. After a split second, Jaime joined him.

Paxton barked, "Lance Corporal MacWha!" but Hawthorne said, "Let him go." He turned to Caitlin. "Why take that little kernel when the crown is a hundred meters away in your tent?"

"The crown is stored in a specially-made iron box," she replied. "I suspect the drone didn't detect it."

"Any idea why they took the kernel?" Hawthorne asked.

"None. Kevin?"

He'd buttoned his pants but was still sitting in the dirt. "Maybe because the biometal is supposed to be in earth's lithosphere, not on the surface? It's dangerous, or has been until now."

"We could ask," Lizbeth said. "I mean, since they can't lie…"

"The problem with asking questions is they often reveal what *we* know," Seamus said.

Lizbeth nodded in agreement. "But what if we know more than they do? I mean about the history of the Ir and the Omnipresent? It's been a crazy long time."

"True," Seamus said after a moment's thought. "Countless regimes could have risen and fallen between then and now, but whether or not the aliens are aware of the sphere network's origin, they *are* still using it."

Tara spoke up tentatively. "Did anyone else notice that—that tingly feelin' coming from the drone?"

"I did," Lizbeth said. "Felt like being near the crown."

Kevin got to his feet and brushed his hands over the seat of his pants. "It took the kernel. Maybe it was programmed to collect every sample of the biometal it encountered."

"If so, it's yet another thing our alien visitors neglected to mention," Hawthorne said.

Chapter Fifteen

Flamborough, England

Zach raced after the drone but couldn't follow it beyond the edge of the chalk cliff. It didn't float straight across to the alien ships; instead it traveled vertically down the cliff face. Its passage must have disrupted some of the birds nesting on the cliff, because a cloud of seabirds filled the air.

Zach wanted nothing more than to strip down and shift into one of them, but even if he could figure out how, he certainly didn't know how to fly.

Jaime skidded to a stop next to him. "Where'd it go?"

"Down the cliff."

Jaime dropped to his belly and crawled forward on his elbows until his head hung past the edge. "Can't see it."

"It's there."

"I wish I could change into a goat or somethin'."

Zach laughed. "I was thinking bird."

Jaime got to his feet. "Yeah, that'd be better. Speaking of, where's Caw?"

Zach studied the flock of seabirds but didn't spot one with all-black feathers among them. Caw always seemed to know when he needed him, but the raven was nowhere to be seen. A wave of anxiety swept through him. He'd snuck Caw a bit of the tainted chicken, and then later had coaxed the bird to land briefly on the crown when no one was looking. It had never occurred to him that Caw's metabolism might work differently, or that what he'd done might hurt his avian friend. But he hadn't seen him all morning, not even after breakfast outside the mess tent, where Caw usually took up residence to beg scraps off the soldiers.

"There it is!" Jaime said, pointing out at the waves.

For a second, Zach thought he meant Caw, but then he spotted the drone offshore, hovering above the waves on a beeline for the alien ships.

The disturbed seabirds cried raucously. One of them dipped and banked sharply, chased by several others of its kind. For a brief, disorienting moment Zach felt as if he was seeing through the bird's eyes: the cliff, the other birds – and the drone, surrounded by a bluish haze – all in a near 360-degree field of view. When he saw himself standing next to Jaime, a wave of vertigo hit, not unlike the feeling of spinning out of control in a tilt-a-whirl.

His vision cleared just as the bird suddenly changed course and flew straight for him, slanting sideways at the last second to allow its wingspan to fit between Zach and Jaime. The birds on its tail ceased pursuit rather than fly near the humans. Just as a niggle of suspicion wormed its way into Zach's mind, he felt the familiar sensation of a bird's claws strike his shoulder from behind.

"Uh, Zach..." Jaime said.

Zach twisted his neck to get a better look at the feathered passenger on his shoulder. He didn't know what color the other seabirds' eyes were, but this one had blue irises just like Caw.

"Seriously?" he said to the bird. "You figured out how to shift before us? You little turd-brain."

Caw nuzzled Zach's cheek with the top of his head.

Zach scratched the base of the short feathers near his beak, murmuring, "You even know how to change back?"

To Zach's astonishment, Caw fluffed his feathers and shifted into his own form.

"Whoa," Jaime drawled. "When did *that* happen?"

"I may have given him some chicken and encouraged him to land on the crown when no one was paying attention."

Jaime started to reply, but Zach inhaled sharply as something occurred to him. Slowly, so he wouldn't disturb the bird, he lowered himself to the ground, folding his legs into a comfortable cross-legged position. He took a couple of slow breaths in through his nose and out through his mouth, relaxing into a pre-meditative state.

"What are ya doin'?" Jaime asked.

"Trying to see through Caw's eyes."

53

"Can ya do that?"

"Pretty sure it just happened, actually."

"Wow." Jaime sat next to him and settled into silence.

Zach reached into his pocket and pulled out the hunk of oatmeal raisin scone he'd saved from breakfast. Caw leaned forward eagerly, claws gripping Zach's hoodie. Normally, Zach would just let the bird take the entire hunk, but he wanted Caw to hang around, so he fed him little bits as he tried to reconnect.

Caitlin had prepped the initiates on what to expect. She'd given them a rundown on what they would and would not be able to do with their new abilities, and approximately when. She'd discussed their gossamers – the magnetic fields produced by electrical activity in the brain – which they would be able to use to read other people's minds. Newbies would be limited to getting mental impressions from people with whom they had direct eye contact. Only adepts could access the minds of those not standing within a few feet, and even then, there were limitations. Not once had Caitlin mentioned that Zach's gossamers might allow him to see through another's eyes, much less at a distance with zero eye contact.

Zach kept reaching out to Caw with his gossamers to the best of his newfound ability, but the bird was fully engaged in eating.

"Anything?" Jaime asked.

"Nah. Maybe I imagined it."

"Or maybe Caw's the one that did it."

"What do you mean?"

Jaime shrugged. "Those other birds were chasing him. Maybe he wanted to get your attention. You are part of his murder."

"Huh?"

"A flock of crows is called a murder."

"Caw's a raven."

"Same difference." Jaime reached a hand out to Caw and was rewarded with a sharp peck on the thumb.

"Ow!" Jaime laughed. "Thanks a lot."

Caw finished the scone and launched off Zach's shoulder, heading away from the cliff. Zach tried and failed one last time to merge with the bird's gossamers, before he gave up and got to his feet. "We should probably get back."

Chapter Sixteen

Flamborough, England

Kevin sat in the command tent half-listening as the members of the Welcoming Committee discussed the latest events. He'd been fighting a strange feeling ever since the drone took the kernel, almost as if he'd forgotten something. He didn't know if it stemmed from loss of the kernel itself or what.

"So where's Caw now?" Hawthorne asked.

Kevin hadn't been paying attention enough to know why Hawthorne was asking after the raven, but he listened to Zach's answer, "Off being a bird, I guess."

"Well, can you call him?"

"I could, but he'd probably just ignore me."

"Try," Caitlin said.

Zach made a wry face but scooted his chair away from the table and stood. Before he took one step towards the tent opening, Caw flew in and landed on his shoulder.

"There's definitely a connection there," Bill said.

"He's always sort of known when I needed him," Zach responded. "Been my 'eye in the sky' for a while now, except, you know, he can't tell me what he sees other than counting."

"Counting?" Hawthorne asked.

"Yeah, I mean, he'll caw to tell me how many people are in a building, for instance. I was thinking if he flew out to the ships, maybe we could reconnoiter them."

"Every military organization on the planet has studied those ships exhaustively from every angle and spectrum," Hawthorne replied. "What could Caw see that they haven't?"

"It's not what he might see," Caitlin said, "but what we might see through his eyes."

Kevin looked at Caw, still trying to figure out what he'd missed. See through Caw's eyes?

"It's a moot point if Zach can't figure out how to do it again," Hawthorne said.

Zach sat back down in his chair across from Kevin, and Caw settled on his shoulder. "Maybe Kevin can tap into the sphere to give me a boost or something."

Everyone looked at Kevin, who pinched the bridge of his nose between thumb and forefinger wearily. "Sorry. I spaced out. What are we talking about?"

"Caw's one of us," Zach said. "I initiated him on the sly to see what would happen. He was flying earlier, and I saw what he saw."

Kevin regarded Caw thoughtfully for a moment. Some time ago, he'd mimicked the sounds the bird made in an attempt to get him to cooperate. It had worked; something he attributed at the time to dumb luck, but now he wondered about that. He'd always been strangely adept at languages, but he'd never tried to actually 'talk' to an animal before.

"Kevin," Lizbeth said.

"Yeah, uh…hold on a sec."

He attempted to catch Caw's eye, but the bird was busy looking around the room – probably for anything that resembled food. Kevin slapped the table to get his attention, and as soon as Caw's head turned, reached out with his gossamers. In an instant, Kevin knew. From deep in his throat, he forced a croaking sound.

Caw tilted his head and then jumped off Zach's shoulder onto the table. Three short hops brought him within inches of Kevin's hand. Caw made a scratchy sound and Kevin chuckled.

"He's hungry. Pretty sure he'd like some aged carrion."

"What, are you Dr. Doolittle now?" Zach sounded annoyed. "How much could a bird have to say?"

"Actually," Kevin said drily, "I suspect he's got a surprisingly robust vocabulary."

"Robust enough to understand if you ask how I saw through his eyes?"

56

"No, he doesn't understand any of that. How could he? But once *you* figure out how you did it, I'm pretty sure he'll do what I ask him to – as long as we offer him a tasty reward."

"This is genuinely fascinating," Hawthorne said, "but I'm still not convinced the bird will be of much assistance."

Seamus leaned forward and linked his fingers together. "Maybe he won't, but I can't see the harm. It's better than sitting here waiting for them to initiate contact again."

"And *that*," Caitlin jumped in, "is the crux of my latest concern. What reason could they have to avoid an open dialog with us? Kevin told them we were frightened, so why leave us to stew in our terror?"

"So we don't ask questions," Lizbeth said.

Caitlin touched a finger to her nose to indicate that Lizbeth's comment was on the mark. "Since they cannot lie to us, avoidance is the next best thing."

"Deception by omission." Seamus turned to Kevin. "They do have a word for omit...?"

Kevin nodded slowly. "And I know it's not terribly helpful, but I have a strange feeling that we're...missing something."

"Given the lack of information, I'm sure we're missing plenty," Bill said.

"That's not what I meant. It's more like...an emptiness. And it's getting stronger."

Chapter Seventeen

Flamborough, England

Caw had always been free to come and go, but he didn't seem to notice or mind when they brought him into the tent they'd been assigned and zipped up the flap. Jaime had scrounged up a roll of duct tape and repaired the slit Zach had cut in the tough fabric, so the tent was effectively an enclosure to prevent the bird from leaving.

Lizbeth settled next to Zach on his cot as Caw and Kevin 'talked.' The conversation was mostly one-sided, since Kevin had a hard time mimicking the raven's vocalizations. Caw seemed to be taking the whole 'communicating with humans' thing in stride, although the majority of what he considered important enough to discuss was food-centric. Occasionally, he would 'say' something else, though. He'd perched on the tent's crossbar and had just made a loud, hollow "*bronk!*" sound that Kevin loosely interpreted as, "I'm King of the Mountain."

Lizbeth exchanged grins with Tara, Tainie and Jaime at that, but Zach didn't seem to hear it. He'd been uncharacteristically quiet for the half hour they'd been conversing with Caw, while he tried to re-form the elusive connection that had occurred on the cliff.

"Ask him what his favorite food is," Tainie said.

"No, don't," Zach snapped. "Would it be asking too much to get a little help here? This isn't a game."

"How can we help?" Lizbeth said. "We weren't there. We don't know what happened."

"I told you what happened."

Lizbeth tilted her head, gaze fixed on his face. "Tell us again."

Zach closed his eyes, jutting his jaw forward. "The drone had just gone down the side of the..." His eyes opened. "The drone."

"What about it?" Jaime asked.

Zach looked at Kevin, a pained look on his face. "Lizbeth mentioned you thought the drones were collecting any loose biometal they found. Well, when I saw through Caw's eyes, I caught a glimpse of the one that took the kernel – and it had a bluish haze around it, like an energy field."

Kevin's eyebrows rose. "You think Caw can see the energy from the biometal?"

"What else could it be?"

"Maybe it was a force field," Tainie said. "Remember those Kentucky hunters who said their bullets disappeared?"

"Or," Kevin said, "They might be tapping into the gossamer sphere itself and using Earth's magnetic field as a power source. That would explain the weird feeling I've been getting, like the sphere is getting weaker."

"Remember how many birds died after the poles reversed?" Tainie asked. "There's this theory that migratory birds can see magnetic fields, and the scientists thought that was why they all died, because they lost their way."

"Are ravens even migratory birds?" Jaime asked.

"No idea," Zach said. "But I know what I saw – or what Caw saw. Anyway, what if the reason I could see through his eyes was because of the drone's proximity?"

Kevin jumped up and walked over to Caitlin's cot. He squatted down and pulled the box with the gossamer crown out from under it. He opened the box and said, "Try now."

Zach frowned up at Caw and a split second later gasped. Lizbeth put her hand on his knee, and suddenly her field of vision changed – she was looking down on the occupants of the tent, who were all bathed in the silvery-blue glow emanating from the gossamer crown.

Chapter Eighteen

Silverpit Crater, the North Sea

Zach jumped out of the helicopter, boots hitting the tarmac as wind from the still-spinning blades plastered his clothes to his body. He raised a hand to place it on Caw's folded wings, worried the bird might try to fly before it was safe.

The entire Welcoming Committee had been flown out to the aircraft carrier USS Harry S. Truman, part of the American battle fleet maintaining position a kilometer from the alien ships. There were about two dozen jets on the flight deck, and from the look of the sailors, the general feeling was one of heightened tension.

"Let's go!" General Hawthorne waved for them to follow him towards a group waiting near the control tower.

For the first time since Zach had met Caitlin that fateful day in San Francisco, he felt like he had an integral part to play. He walked between Lizbeth and Kevin, head held high.

Hawthorne greeted the commander of the Truman and his officers and gave them a brief rundown on their mission.

The afternoon light was fading fast. As soon as Hawthorne gave the word, Kevin spoke to Caw and the bird launched from Zach's shoulder. Zach watched until Caw was a black speck in the sky.

Caitlin opened the box holding the gossamer crown and removed it. When she placed the crown on her head, Zach had a flashback to the day they'd stopped the Cataclysm. They'd been on a ship in the North Sea then, too, albeit a much smaller one.

This time, after we save the earth, he thought, *the whole world will know about it.* He didn't even entertain the notion that they might not succeed.

He took Caitlin's proffered hand in one of his, and Lizbeth's in the other. The rest of the Welcoming Committee joined hands, too, until they were all linked physically and mentally. The connection made him feel invincible and brought to mind his mother's declaration that he had da Zhuang – great power. For the first time since his initiation, Zach felt that power flowing through and around him. What he'd only had hints of before was now a stunning reality.

No longer awkward and unsure, he reached out with his gossamers and despite the distance between them, instantly connected with Caw. Moments later, he felt the others connect to Caw's visual field. The bird had yet to reach his goal, but he was close enough for Zach to see clearly what he'd been unable to before: a vast orb of bluish energy encompassing the alien ships.

A force field.

The three massive ships themselves were still hovering well above the water equidistant to each other. As Caw got closer, it became apparent that something was happening; something that had been blocked not only from their human eyesight, but from that of every instrument focused on the trio of ships. Suspended in midair between the ships was another force field, and within that floated a dull metallic ball, and even as Zach watched, material from beneath the waves flowed upwards, adding to its mass.

In the past, whenever the Fae used their gossamers to communicate, it had been impossible to determine who was speaking, or to glean emotion from their words. When Kevin sent the message, *"They're taking the gossamer sphere!"* it was not only clear who'd sent it, but his rage was almost palpable.

A rapid-fire conversation ensued.

Seamus: *"This is why they refused to talk to us."*

Kevin: *"I knew something was wrong."*

Lizbeth: *"I thought they couldn't lie."*

Zach: *"Yeah, unless they removed the word 'lie' from their vocabulary to fool us into thinking they couldn't."*

Hawthorne: *"What will happen if they take the sphere?"*

Caitlin: *"We will lose the bulk of our abilities."*

Bill: *"Earth will be helpless."*

Paxton: *"How much of it have they taken?"*

A surge of energy coursed through Zach's body just before Kevin sent: "*Not enough to stop us from taking it back.*"

Zach heard a commotion outside of their internal conversation. Someone was shouting, but he didn't need to hear the words to know what the problem was. He was still connected to Caw, and through the bird's eyes saw a number of apertures on the alien ships open, allowing small aircraft to launch in all directions. These were not the slow, methodical beetle-drones, but were shaped like three-bladed arrowheads spinning through the air with such speed they were a blur.

One of them headed straight for Caw, who tucked his wings and dove below it. The arrowhead didn't bother swinging back around, but that's not what told Zach the bird had not been its target. No, he learned that when the arrowhead streaked towards one of the thousands of boats and ships in the area and shot a fiery blue orb at it.

Tara let out a little shriek as the boat exploded.

"Oh, my God," Jaime said.

In the background, someone screamed, "We are under attack! Repeat, *we are under attack!*"

"*Now what?*" Zach's stomach felt like it was tied up in knots.

"*It can't be a coincidence that they attacked right after we found out what they're up to,*" Seamus sent.

"*Which tells us two things,*" Kevin responded. "*They're watching us, and they think we can stop them.*"

"*We should consider this is a distraction,*" Caitlin sent. "*They want to keep us occupied while they continue to summon the biometal.*"

Some distraction, Zach thought dazedly.

The majority of the arrowheads joined in the attack on the boats, but a contingent of about thirty sped straight for the Truman. One of the sailors yelled, "Incoming!"

Zach snapped back to his own visual field as someone shoved him from behind. "Get them below!"

"No!" Hawthorne cried. "We stay here!"

Zach looked around. Men in flight suits were scrambling for their jets. A barrage of *boom-boom-booms* reverberated like thunder as the big guns on the ships surrounding the Truman began to defend the carrier.

"Kevin," Hawthorne said, "the energy column you created in the auditorium to block the signal from Agent Collins' detonator – can you do that to protect the boats?"

"Yes, sir," Kevin said grimly.

Caitlin sent, *"Don't disconnect, any of you. Kevin needs our support."*

"Take as much as you need, bro." Zach had never been Kevin's biggest fan, but in this moment, to save the world – again – he would die for him. They were now and forever connected.

Chapter Nineteen

Silverpit Crater, the North Sea

Kevin stared at the crown on Caitlin's head, focusing hard on the triskele symbol – the key to accessing the sphere's power. When his mind merged with the silver stream, he sensed that the strength of the sphere had been significantly minimized. The aliens had taken less than a quarter of the biometal, but the grid itself, deep in the lithosphere, must still be intact. If the grid broke, and it was only a matter of time before it did, Kevin and the others would be powerless.

He connected with Caw's gossamers. The bird was close enough to land on the nearest alien ship, but for some reason, hadn't done so. Instead, he circled around it above the force field. That was fine by Kevin, who used Caw's visual field to pinpoint the boats that had yet to be destroyed by the arrowheads.

As quickly as he could, he pulled column after column of energy from beneath the earth's crust. The columns stretched high into the sky, tapering off somewhere beyond earth's atmosphere. Each one fully encompassed a boat, and Kevin hoped none of the passengers were descendants of the Fae; otherwise they would be frozen in place like Zach and General Hawthorne had been, unable to move or breathe.

"*How can we help?*" Lizbeth sent.

None of the others knew how to form the energy columns, and Kevin wasn't creating them fast enough. In desperation, he attempted to mentally condense the process and broadcast it to all of them. He knew he'd succeeded when Zach said, "Whoa."

"*Excellent,*" Caitlin sent. "*Well done, Kevin.*" She and the others began protecting the boats.

The odor of fuel exhaust was strong. The jets weren't in the air yet but would be any moment. Hawthorne spoke aloud. "The battleships won't be able to hold the arrowheads off the Truman forever. Can we put a column around it?"

"If we do," Kevin replied, "the jets won't be able to take off."

"I'll try to get the captain to abort their launch." Hawthorne left the circle and strode off towards the control tower.

"*If we protect the Truman, won't that cut us off from the outside?*" Seamus sent.

"*Yes. We should split up.*" Caitlin looked around the circle. "*Zach, Jaime?*"

Zach knew exactly what she had in mind. "*Can you do that thing Kevin just did and teach us to fly?*"

While Caitlin attempted that, Hawthorne bellowed, "Tell the air boss not to launch! Repeat, do *not* launch the aircraft!"

Zach and Jaime, armed with the knowledge Caitlin sent them, left the circle. They stripped off their clothes and shifted. Even though the condor was one of the world's largest birds, the two young men were several times larger. To make up for the difference, their wingspans were longer, but they were still unable to take off.

"*Run!*" Caitlin sent. "*Launch off the side of the carrier!*"

With huge wings partially spread, Zach and Jaime ran, hopped, and glided short distances until they reached the side of the Truman. As they leapt off, the first jet roared across the flight deck.

"*New plan,*" Kevin sent. "*Don't put columns around the Truman or the battleships in the fleet. Let's hope they can hold the arrowheads off.*"

Chapter Twenty

Silverpit Crater, the North Sea

Another jet took to the sky, and Lizbeth silently cheered when the pilots engaged the nearest arrowheads and shot one down. From her connection to Hawthorne, she knew he'd given up trying to talk the Americans out of engaging the enemy. Instead, he'd gotten on the com to the Royal Air Force to request backup.

Another group of arrowheads were within firing distance, kept at bay by the heavy artillery coming from the other ships in the carrier fleet.

Lizbeth glanced at Kevin, who seemed to have tuned out. She knew what he was doing; knew how necessary it was to keep the aliens from removing their source of power, but without his guidance…

No, she interrupted her own thoughts. *Kevin isn't the only one who can figure out what needs to be done.*

Her father had been Fae, a man who'd used his secret abilities to become a celebrated magician. He'd taught his only child how to do any number of tricks, including how to pick pockets. There were several key strategies to becoming a successful pickpocket, but the most important was to have a soft touch. In and out before the mark could even begin to suspect what she was up to. It had been Lizbeth's particular talent, a talent that on the surface had no place in this fight.

Even as a way to potentially use that talent occurred to her, an explosion rocked the ship. She clapped her hands over her ears to muffle the deafening sound of it. Black smoke drifted across her field of vision, and she closed her eyes to think.

The arrowheads were extremely fast, and to Lizbeth's untrained eye, had unprecedented maneuvering capabilities. They easily avoided the many energy columns protecting the boats, weaving between and around them. It struck her that if the arrowheads were unable to dodge those columns, it would be like smashing into a brick wall. There was only one way she could think of to make that happen, and it relied on a few assumptions, the first being that the arrowheads were not unmanned, and that the alien pilots had something similar to gossamers for her to latch onto. She was somewhat confident that this assumption was true, because at least one alien species in the consortium had spoken mind-to-mind with Kevin. Even if they *were* using technology to make that happen, there had to be a conduit. Some way for their thoughts to connect with that technology.

She was more confident about her second assumption: that the added power of the circle would boost the strength of her gossamers. The circle had already extended her gossamers' reach, since she'd easily connected with Caw, so hopefully her assumption would prove correct.

She took a deep breath and focused on the key, the triskele symbol. She reached out with her gossamers, beyond the circle, beyond the Truman itself. After a short amount of time without sensing anything or anyone, she drew more power from the circle and tried to spread her gossamers out, visualizing them as more of a blanket than tendrils of electromagnetic current.

That worked, but only minimally. She sensed the human pilots whenever a jet flew through her gossamer blanket, and she also sensed a foreign presence coming from the arrowheads, but the contact came and went far too rapidly for her to connect with it. She tried adding a third dimension to her gossamer blanket, drawing still more power from the circle. That attracted Caitlin's attention, but her grandmother didn't ask what she was doing – she just sort of hovered as an onlooker, waiting to act.

Lizbeth's gossamers were now 'thick' enough for her to inspect the foreign presences inside the arrowheads that passed through it, but nothing about those presences suggested sentience. It reminded her of the iron-lined hats the MI6 agents had all been wearing. The hats kept the agents' gossamers contained so that whenever she'd reached out towards one of them, all she'd sensed was…life…as if she'd tried to read an amoeba or something.

She opened her eyes and turned to Caitlin. "*Do you think they know? Are they wearing iron-lined helmets?*"

"They've had days to study us. Even if they don't know the legend of the Ir and the Omnipresent, they could have seen the footage from the auditorium. It's highly likely they do *know iron is our weakness."*

Lizbeth fought against a wave of panic. Men were screaming all around her. The ship beneath her feet shook from another direct hit that tore up the flight deck. No more jets would be able to launch. The air was hot and acrid, but she kept on breathing, slowly, calmly, focused on the problem like her father had taught her.

Just because the aliens were wearing iron-lined helmets didn't mean she couldn't latch onto their gossamers – she'd just have to come at them from a different direction. Caitlin had once told her that the old adage, 'The eyes are the window to the soul' was particularly true for Fae. Lizbeth had no desire to see into the aliens' souls, but, as she and the others had recently learned with Caw, sometimes it worked the other way around. A pilot's helmet might protect whatever passed for its brain, but presumably its sight would need to remain unrestricted.

She closed her eyes again and sent her gossamers out. Moments later she felt that weird presence, and she clung to it like a burr to a sock. She probed deeper, sending delicate little licks of her gossamers inward, following and retreating back through branches of electrical impulses that indicated she'd accessed its neurological system. The more she probed, the more feedback she got about this particular life form. Whenever her gossamers brushed against the iron, there was no feedback at all, which was telling in its own way. Soon enough she had a rough map of the pilot's bizarre physical structure.

Where are your eyes, you disgusting little creep? she thought. *Ah...there.*

Suddenly she was in. Her own eyes were closed, but she saw a strange instrument panel before her; at its center, the Truman between glowing blue crosshairs. She knew the pilot was about to fire. Caitlin knew it too, and Lizbeth sensed her intention just before Caitlin pulled a column of energy from the earth directly in the pilot's path. Lizbeth withdrew from its mind before the arrowhead collided with the silver column and disintegrated in a dazzling flash of blue light.

Chapter Twenty-one

Silverpit Crater, the North Sea

Flying was exhilarating. From the moment Zach jumped off the side of the aircraft carrier and the wind caught his outstretched wings and lifted him, he felt as though he were on the thrill ride of a lifetime. If he had human vocal cords, he would have let loose with a fervent, "Woooo!" As it was, he only had a brief moment to enjoy the sensation before his 'birds-eye' view of the devastation sobered him up.

He was still connected to the group on the Truman and heard that Hawthorne was unable to stop the jets from taking off. It seemed they hadn't needed to split up after all, and for a moment, he considered turning back, but something indefinable urged him onward.

He swept his wings down in great beats that sent him ever higher, Jaime trailing behind.

"*Shouldn't we go back?*" Jaime sent.

"*You can if you want. I'm going to get a look at the ships.*"

"*Why?*"

Zach had no idea why he felt drawn towards the aliens, but he came up with a logical reason on the fly, "*Because if the Truman goes down, everyone on board dies and humanity loses. End of story.*"

Kevin and the others continued to erect columns of energy, so Zach and Jaime were careful to avoid flying directly over any boats that had yet to be protected. Several times, arrowheads zipped on past them, but the pilots didn't seem to consider the two huge birds a threat, because they were ignored.

Zach's condor eyesight was similar to Caw's, and as they approached the three alien ships, he was perfectly able to see the orb of bluish energy surrounding them. He recalled that when Caitlin and Seamus had gotten too close, they'd lost their ability to shift.

"*We need to stay away from that energy field,*" he sent to Jaime.

"*Copy that.*"

They flew up and up until the air grew thin and cold. From this height, the destruction the arrowheads had wrought was far away, but no less horrifying. Zach saw an arrowhead get a shot off that hit the Truman and a shaft of fear ran through him until he realized he could still sense Lizbeth and the others. Soon after that, the first arrowhead crashed into a column that Caitlin had deliberately erected in its path. Zach cheered internally and exulted as more and more of the enemy were defeated in this way.

"*What's that?*" Jaime sent.

Zach didn't know what Jaime was referring to until he spotted a far-off object in the southeastern sky, a trail of white smoke in its wake. At first, he thought it was merely a passenger aircraft with a contrail, but then Hawthorne responded, "*Carrier air traffic control says bogeys are popping up all over the radar. This is not the cavalry, people. Those are missiles, and they're coming from countries with nuclear arms. It'll all be over in minutes. For us anyway.*"

Zach flapped his wings, fighting despair. Even if they could surround each of the missiles with a column of energy, once the columns were taken down, which would happen as soon as the biometal grid broke, nuclear fallout and climate change would kill everyone on the planet. As his fellow Fae discussed their options, all he could think about was Lizbeth – how he'd never gotten a chance to tell her how he felt.

He didn't get a chance now, either. He and Jaime had just flown over the closest alien ship and a glance downward told him the arrowheads were heading back to their hangars. A partially formed thought – that the aliens were hunkering down to wait it out behind their force field while the humans destroyed their own world – was interrupted when the fin of a passing arrowhead glanced off one of Jaime's wings.

Black feathers twirled through the air like maple seeds falling from a tree, and Jaime, too, spun out of control. Zach dove after him, knowing as he did so that Jaime's body was far too heavy for him to carry in flight. It turned out to be a moot point, since before Zach got close enough to try, the energy field surrounding the alien ships stripped them of their shifting ability.

70

In human form, they plummeted towards the ball of biometal suspended between the ships. Instinctively, Zach prepared himself for a rough landing – not that a standard tuck and roll would save him from this height.

Chapter Twenty-two

Silverpit Crater, the North Sea

In the past, when Kevin had retrieved the microscopic biometal from the drill ship core sample and from Tara's mine, all he'd had to do was concentrate. At his behest, the metal had demonstrated its living qualities by becoming fluid and flowing towards his hand, reforming into a solid kernel in his palm. It had been nearly effortless on his part; all he'd had to do was ask.

Now when he asked, nothing happened. The aliens had seized control of the biometal somehow.

The arrowheads were all heading back to their mother ships, but Kevin suspected the aliens were not on the verge of retreating. On the contrary, a drain on the power emanating from the gossamer sphere told him they were gearing up for something – they probably needed the power to strengthen the force field surrounding their ships.

If only he knew more about them. He'd been the one who'd inadvertently initiated contact, but he'd done it while asleep, and his memory of the events seemed like a dream. Had there even been an exchange of information? He'd originally thought so, but really had no idea. Just like the message from Queen Wyn, he had access to only bits and pieces of it. If only he could unlock his own mind…

Kevin sucked in a breath. He was surrounded by chaos and yet suddenly felt as if he were in suspended animation, floating between worlds.

The triskele symbol.

With no hesitation, he summoned it to mind, and in the blink of an eye, the knowledge that had been hovering at the edge of his consciousness became clear. There hadn't been a conversation. The aliens had plumbed his mind for information with no intention of reciprocating. They'd learned all they could about his world, and about the Fae.

Luckily, they'd done so before he got the message from Wyn.

With a feeling of both chagrin and triumph, he visualized the key again. Wyn's message – *the Ir's message* – which had been sitting in his mind like a textbook he had to slowly thumb through, suddenly unlocked in its entirety.

The Ir rebels had chronicled everything they knew about their enemy. What Kevin took away from the information was that anything Omnipresent technology could accomplish using the biometal was also possible for the Fae.

"*Listen!*" he broadcast to everyone. "*We can stop the missiles, but we need more power, so we have to pull down the columns around the boats. Lizbeth! Get into one of the arrowhead pilots' heads before they're all behind the force field. Use the triskele symbol! It's the key to everything. I need you to find a schematic of their ship so we can stop them from taking the rest of the biometal. The rest of you, hang on. We've got work to do.*"

Chapter Twenty-three

Silverpit Crater, the North Sea

Lizbeth reached out with her gossamers and latched onto the nearest alien pilot, entering through its eyes like a hammer striking a nail. Its mind was wholly inhuman, and its thought process completely foreign. Even as she struggled to understand it, she saw through its eyes as it piloted the arrowhead towards the alien ship furthest away from the Truman. Just as she was about to disconnect from its visual field and probe deeper into its mind, she saw Zach and Jaime plunge into the silvery mass of biometal. They didn't hit it – they simply disappeared into it as if it were made of gelatin.

She screamed, disrupting the connection with the alien and yanking her gossamers out of its mind. Before the echo of her cry could fade away, Caitlin sent, "*Lizbeth! Focus. Think of your mother, your grandmother. If we fail, they die, too. There will time to grieve later.*"

With tears streaming down her face, Lizbeth found and punched her way into another alien pilot's mind but had no idea how to find the information Kevin had asked for. Unlike Kevin, she didn't speak the pilot's language. She flailed around in its mind as the seconds ticked by, getting nothing but impressions that made no sense. It occurred to her that even if she understood the alien psyche, the pilot might not have access to the ships' schematics. That was when she remembered that Kevin had told her to use the key. She pictured the triskele symbol and sent a question blindly into the pilot's mind.

"*How do your ships work?*"

To her astonishment, her question was immediately answered. Bizarre designs spooled through her mind.

"*Kevin!*" she sent. "*Will this help?*"

"*Got it,*" he replied. "*Okay, wow. This is all very similar to Omnipresent technology.*"

Lizbeth retreated from the alien's mind – just in time, as it happened. There were a few dozen arrowheads that had yet to penetrate the shield surrounding the mother ships. Every one of them unexpectedly exploded, showering burning debris over the boats directly beneath them.

"What the hell...?" Hawthorne exclaimed.

"*They know we breached their security,*" Caitlin sent, "*so they destroyed the arrowheads we still had access to.*"

Lizbeth glanced around outside of the circle. Sailors were scrambling to put out fires. Two of the four jets that had launched had been shot down, and the remaining two were unable to land on the Truman due to the damage to the flight deck. The wind was blowing the smoke away, so she was able to look up at the grey post-Cataclysm sky. Incoming missiles were everywhere.

"Did the schematics help?" she asked.

He grinned. "I'm sure they will, but first we have to take care of those missiles."

Lizbeth let out a breath she didn't know she'd been holding.

"How?" Hawthorne demanded.

Kevin closed his eyes, and a moment later, the information appeared in Lizbeth's mind. The columns of energy they'd created were the easiest way to make use of earth's magnetic field. Creating a hollow, transparent energy sphere exactly like the one encompassing the alien ships was more complicated, but once they knew how, everyone in the circle began forming them around the missiles. Once a missile was trapped inside, it struck the interior wall of the energy field and detonated, but the force of the blast was completely contained. Then it was a simple matter of pulling a column up underneath the energy sphere, and pushing it into space, where it eventually dissipated.

One by one, the Welcoming Committee dealt with the missiles. It was an arduous process, because they just kept on coming. Lizbeth was shaking with exhaustion, and a crowd of sailors had formed around the circle by the time the last missile had been dispatched. The sailors cheered when it left the atmosphere.

With the latest crisis averted, Lizbeth's fragmented thoughts turned to Zach.

Chapter Twenty-four

Silverpit Crater, the North Sea

Zach's surprise at sinking into the ball of biometal rather than smashing into it was quickly replaced by panic. His first instinct was to 'swim' to the surface, but like quicksand, the more he struggled, the deeper he sank. Blind and deaf, he could do nothing to help himself.

Suffocation was inevitable.

The specter of death had never frightened him, but the reality was a different story. He relaxed his body and tried to calm his mind, hoping to find peace in his last moments, but Jaime's fear made it impossible. Zach could not only sense Jaime's state of mind, but it seemed to be magnified by the biometal, battering against Zach's efforts at tranquility.

As the pressure to breathe mounted and dread began to set in, he decided to fast-track it before he completely lost control. He bent his head back and opened his mouth. The biometal oozed in, tasting like blood. He fought against instinct and inhaled. He expected his lungs to violently spasm as the biometal filled them – but that didn't happen. Instead, his consciousness slipped into focus, and he became aware of his body on an entirely new level as the biometal traveled from his lungs to his blood stream, suffusing his circulatory system and permeating every organ, every cell.

Zach not only found it no longer necessary to breathe, but the urge to do so was gone. His chest settled into stillness. The biometal surrounding him had become an extension of himself, and as if Jaime were a fly caught in his web, he felt the young man's convulsive, panicked movements begin to slow.

"*Breathe it in, bro!*" he sent. "*It won't hurt you!*"

Jaime didn't respond. His fear was fading, and Zach realized he was on the verge of passing out. Whether Jaime would then inhale reflexively, he had no idea, but he couldn't risk doing nothing and letting him die.

Zach extended an arm towards him, knowing Jaime was too far away, but also knowing that he would reach him anyway. In response to his need, Zach's body absorbed more and more biometal, growing in size until his fingertips touched Jaime's arm. He grasped it tightly, his huge hand wrapping around Jaimie's arm like it was a stick. He yanked. *"Breathe! You hear me? Do it* now, *soldier!"*

Jaime must have sucked the biometal into his lungs, because Zach sensed his profound relief. Soon afterward, he felt something brush against his hand and Jaime sent, *"Is that you*?!"

Zach let go of Jaime's arm and laughed in his throat, sending vibrations out through the biometal. *"Big, huh?"*

"Bloody hell. Did you know this would happen?"

"No," Zach replied. *"This is all new territory."*

"How do we get out of this muck?"

"We don't."

By now, the first of the nuclear missiles should have hit. The fact that Zach and Jaime felt nothing meant the aliens' force field was still intact. Zach was almost grateful he hadn't been connected to the others when their mental voices had been silenced.

His heartache was fathomless, but instead of compartmentalizing it, he used it to fuel his white-hot need for vengeance.

Chapter Twenty-five

Silverpit Crater, the North Sea

Kevin looked dazedly around the circle. Everyone was so busy smiling, laughing, hugging – celebrating their victory – that none of them noticed that not long after their victory, the grid of biometal spanning the globe had become too thin to harness earth's magnetic field. To Kevin, it felt as one of his senses had been torn away, leaving his world bereft of depth and substance.

He turned to Tara and saw the triumph fade from her eyes, to be replaced by apprehension. "What is that?"

"We're too late."

"The grid?" Lizbeth's voice was barely above a whisper.

Kevin nodded. "It's broken."

"What do you think they'll do now?" Seamus asked.

"They won't hang around," Kevin replied. "Now that they've taken away our power, they'll find another planet in the solar system – a smaller one, because they don't have all the biometal – and set up a grid there. They don't just use a planet's magnetic field for communication and force fields – it's essential for interstellar travel. According to the message from the Ir, we're way off the beaten path. It took the aliens nine months to get to earth, and they must have come from the nearest outpost."

"So they're trapped in our solar system," Seamus said.

"For the time being. Fat lot of good it does us."

Tara slid her arms around him. "Are they going to leave us alive?"

He pulled her close and laughed humorlessly. "Of course. We're helpless and they've yet to figure out how to use us."

"And the message from the Ir doesn't say how we can defeat them?" Caitlin asked.

"The Ir could only tell us how things were done in their space and time," he said. "The only advantage we seem to have over them is that iron only takes away our power. It killed *them* outright."

Lizbeth sighed, a forlorn sound. "What about the schematics? Can we still take their shield down?"

Kevin shifted his gaze to the alien ships. The force field had blocked the ball of biometal from their view, but now he could see it clearly. "Look. It's already down. They must have been tapping into the grid for extra power."

Hawthorne produced a feral grin. "So they're vulnerable to attack." He turned to one of the officers nearby, who immediately shouted into his com, "Enemy shields are down!"

Kevin had picked up on some of what had been going on around them while they'd dealt with the missiles. Although there were only two American jets still in the air, the British Royal Air Force had launched a squadron. Maybe things weren't entirely hopeless.

He closed his burning eyes for a moment, then opened them and glanced at the alien ships again. His mouth dropped open and he exclaimed, "What the...?"

Everyone in the vicinity turned.

A giant, metallic human hand was pressed against the side of the ball of biometal.

Chapter Twenty-six

Silverpit Crater, the North Sea

Lizbeth had seen a lot of weird things lately, but witnessing Zach and Jaime absorb the biometal they'd fallen into was by far the weirdest. The gigantic hand was followed by the curve of a bare back, and then, as their bodies absorbed the biometal like sponges, legs and feet. When all the biometal was gone, there were two huge metallic bodies curled up next to each other in the fetal position, floating in midair.

"That…that's just…" General Hawthorne was at a loss for words.

Seamus, a look of utter amazement on his face, said, "They're moving, but it's like they're trapped inside an invisible egg."

"Whatever force contained the biometal appears to now be containing *them*," Caitlin said.

Lizbeth felt tears start in her eyes. "We have to help them. If the aliens leave…" she trailed off, but Caitlin finished her sentence, "They'll take the boys with them into space."

"The schematics," Kevin muttered, staring at the tarmac in concentration. "I can't—it's all there, but without the grid…"

Lizbeth thrust her hands out towards the people on either side of her. "Circle!"

Everyone linked hands again. After a moment, Kevin said, "That's better. I got it. General? How far out are those RAF jets?"

"Should be in our airspace any moment now," Hawthorne replied.

Kevin nodded. "We need them to focus their attack on the portion of the ships facing Zach and Jaime. There's a big satellite-dish-looking-thing there. If they can disable one of those, Zach and Jaime should be freed."

"But make sure they don't shoot *them*!" Lizbeth said.

Hawthorne raised his eyebrows and said drily, "Quite," before hurrying off to make the call.

Lizbeth heard a distant roar, like approaching thunder, and looked towards land. As the general had predicted, the British jets were on their way. In a short amount of time, they'd spanned the distance between the coast and the alien ships. She crossed her fingers as the jets fired the first volley of short-range missiles. The alien mother ships fired back, and she stared in horror at the sheer volume of projectiles streaking through the air. Not only were the RAF missiles detonated well short of their targets, but half the jets were taken out, too. She gaped as burning wreckage rained down upon the North Sea. As the remaining jets retreated, she spotted a lone parachute in the sky.

Lizbeth, knees weak, turned to Caitlin, who took her into her arms and hugged her tightly, whispering, "We'll think of something."

Over her grandmother's shoulder, Lizbeth saw the alien ships begin to rise slowly upward, towing Zach and Jaime beneath them.

Chapter Twenty-seven

Silverpit Crater, the North Sea

Zach saw the jets and thought the cavalry had arrived until hundreds of apertures twisted open on the alien ships. He could only watch helplessly as the aliens fired on the jets, easily repelling their offensive.

When the alien ships began to move, he almost went berserk trying to break free from the flexible force holding him suspended above the sea, but no matter how hard he pushed, the force kept him contained. Next to him, Jaime, too, struggled futilely.

Then it occurred to Zach that he was no longer limited to his human form. Lizbeth had shifted into a gorilla, and she'd been easily able to heft his body over her shoulder, so he tried that first. When it didn't work, he tried to think of something stronger, rejecting every animal that came to mind until he flashed back to the second grade, when he'd been fascinated by bugs. Comparatively speaking, certain beetles were the strongest creatures on earth, but he wasn't sure he could shift into one. Reptiles, yes, but bugs?

Caitlin had once told them that the DNA of every plant and animal on earth had a dormant code for shape-shifting characteristics, and she'd also said that as oxygen breathers, the Fae were limited in the shapes they could take. As far as he knew, bugs weren't on the menu, but then again, Caitlin had also told them they couldn't change size, and look at him now. The only thing that made him hesitate was the inevitable loss of mental function. He didn't know how much, if any, higher thinking bugs were capable of, but he didn't have much of a choice.

"*We should shift into beetles,*" he sent to Jaime. "*Strongest creatures on earth.*" And then, because he hadn't been specific enough and didn't want

Jaime to become something innocuous like a Ladybug, he sent, *"You ever see a Rhinoceros Beetle?"*

"'Course I have."

"Good. See you on the other side, bro."

Zach concentrated on the memory of the bug books he'd checked out of the library as a boy. He'd studied Dynastinae from the top of their exoskeletons to the tip of their antennae. He felt himself shifting: head, thorax, abdomen, legs, wings. Next to him, Jaime shifted, too.

Zach found his thoughts sluggish, but his objective was still at the forefront of his mind: *Break free.*

He and Jaime were back-to-back, and they pushed against the force field with all their combined might. Zach's mouthparts worked as he thrust his legs outward, reaching for the nearest alien ship with his claws. It seemed as if the force field was weakening, but then a sudden jolt pulsed painfully through his body, forcing him back into his own form.

"Oh, yeah?" he snarled mentally at the unseen aliens. *"You like zapping people? How about a taste of your own medicine? Jaime! Electric eel!"*

"Brill," Jaime replied.

They shifted, and for a moment, Zach was appalled at the feeling of his slimy body writhing next to Jaime's. He pushed his distaste aside, however, and sent, *"On three! One…two…three!"*

Instinct kicked in. Together, he and Jaime generated a brief, but immensely powerful electric shock. It was the sensation of falling that made him realize they'd successfully disabled the force field. He shifted back into a beetle and lifted his elytra, allowing his underwings to open and stop his fall. Jaime hadn't thought as quickly, though, plummeting into the sea with a great splash.

Zach figured Jaime would swim to the Truman, so he started in that direction, too, but then turned in midair. Maybe it was his beetle brain, or maybe just his natural aggressive tendencies, but he was suddenly overwhelmed with the need to bring the fight to the alien jerks who wanted to destroy his world.

Chapter Twenty-eight

Silverpit Crater, the North Sea

Everyone around Kevin began talking at once, but he just stood there and shook his head in admiration. Zach and Jaime shifting into electric eels to overload the containment field? Ingenious. The metallic beetle – Kevin didn't know whether it was Zach or Jaime – landed on top of one of the mother ships and thrust its long horn into an open aperture, using leverage to remove a section of the ship's exterior as if it were peeling an orange.

The aliens couldn't leave without the biometal, so the mother ships had stopped their upward progress and were hovering in place again. While the beetle continued tearing pieces away with a singular determination, Kevin had an epiphany. He broke into a run, heading for the side of the Truman.

"Kevin!" Tara called after him.

He didn't want to take the time to stop and explain, and without an intact sphere, couldn't very well talk to her mind-to-mind without direct eye contact, so he ignored her. When he reached the railing, he toed off his shoes and stripped off his shirt. She and Lizbeth ran up to him as he was yanking off his socks.

"What are you doing?" Lizbeth asked.

He let his jeans fall down around his ankles but paused with his thumbs under the waistband of his boxers. "Zach and Jaime have the biometal in their bodies."

"Right," Tara said, uncomprehending, and then, "Oh! You want to put it back into the grid! Fix the gossamer sphere!"

"Can you even do that?" Lizbeth asked.

"I hope so. Tell Caitlin." Kevin's modesty wouldn't let him get naked in front of them, so he left his boxers on and climbed onto the railing. He'd planned on shifting into a dolphin, but one glance down told him there was a safety net to catch anyone who went overboard, so instead, he shifted into a condor and launched off the railing. As he took to the air, his boxers fluttered into the sea.

He flew towards the mother ships but didn't get very far before spotting a disturbance in the water, a narrow area of churned foam that gave away the eel's location. He had no idea how he was going to get its attention but hoped the biometal in its body had boosted the strength and reach of its gossamers. He circled above it and sent, *"Zach? Jaime? Can you hear me?"*

Within seconds, a huge, squarish snout broke the surface, and the silvery eel twisted its head and regarded Kevin with one small, milky eye.

"It's Jaime. Is that Kevin?"

Kevin started to respond, but to his surprise, Zach answered him, too. *"I hear ya, bro, but I'm a bit busy at the mo."*

Zach was still tearing chunks out of the ship, which made Kevin wonder: why aren't the aliens trying to stop him? He could think of only one reason why they wouldn't – because they couldn't. The electric shock that had disabled the containment field must have damaged the ships somehow. If he was right, they couldn't fire on Zach, but that state of affairs was unlikely to last. They were probably working to repair the damage, and once they did, they would put every last ounce of effort into regaining the biometal.

Kevin continued to fly in a tight circle above Jaime, thinking furiously. His original intention had been to shift into a sea-creature and accompany Jaime down to Silverpit crater – the gossamer sphere's impact site on the sea floor – to remove the biometal from Jaime's body and put it back into grid. It had seemed like a good idea at the time, but he hadn't considered the fact that the aliens would have access to the resulting power, too. Plus, once the aliens repaired their systems, they would only take the biometal from the grid again.

The ideal solution would be to make the Welcoming Committee stronger without giving the aliens any kind of advantage.

"Jaime," Kevin sent. *"Meet me back at the Truman. And hurry!"*

Chapter Twenty-nine

Silverpit Crater, the North Sea

Lizbeth looked wearily around her as Tara gathered up Kevin's clothing. The black smoke rising from the Truman had faded to white, indicating the fires were under control. The battle fleet had launched inflatable pontoon rescue boats to look for survivors in the water. She thought of the lone pilot who'd ejected from his or her jet an instant before it had been destroyed. A sweeping upward glance told her the pilot was no longer drifting through the air.

The Welcoming Committee, minus General Hawthorne and Colonel Paxton, made their way over to where she and Tara stood at the rail.

"What's Kevin up to now?" Seamus asked.

Lizbeth told them Kevin's idea, but as soon as she'd finished speaking, Kevin himself, still in the shape of a condor, flew down and landed awkwardly at her feet. When he shifted back into his own body, naked as the day he was born, Tara gawked and practically threw his bundle of clothing at him. In another place and time, the scenario might have struck Lizbeth as funny, but under the circumstances, modesty was the least of their worries.

"Change of plans." Kevin yanked his jeans up over his hips, calling out, "Jaime?"

A voice appeared in Lizbeth's head: "*Comin' aboard.*" Startled, she said, "I heard him! I thought we couldn't do that anymore."

Kevin grinned. "It's the biometal. Now, don't freak out, but–"

Lizbeth and several of the others gasped as a huge silvery tentacle suddenly appeared and wrapped itself around the railing. A second tentacle shot forth and swept Bill off his feet before attaching itself to the tarmac with its suckers.

"*Sorry about that!*" Two enormous blobs with eyes rose up on the other side of the rail. "*I can't seem to tell where my arms are if I'm not lookin' at 'em. How are we goin' ta do this?*"

"I'll start." Kevin knelt and put a hand on the nearest tentacle. He took a deep breath, let it out slowly and said quietly, "To me."

Lizbeth watched closely, but nothing seemed to be happening.

"Are you doing it right?" Seamus asked.

Kevin removed his hand and wiped it on his pant leg. "I guess not. Any suggestions?"

"Jaime," Caitlin said. "How did you and Zach absorb the biometal?"

Jaime the octopus regarded her with his strange silver eyes. "*We breathed it in.*"

"Really?" Lizbeth asked.

"*True fact*," Jaime responded. "*And now we don't have to breathe at all.*"

"That's because you're more biometal than human," Caitlin said. "I've been thinking about that – how one of the differences between us and the Ir is that we have iron in our blood, which carries the oxygen we breathe to our organs. I believe that's why iron doesn't kill us like it did them."

"It still disables us," Seamus pointed out.

Kevin straightened up and frowned at Jaime. "You and Zach were surrounded by the biometal. We can't very well breathe–"

He didn't finish his sentence because the tentacle he'd touched lifted from the deck and slapped him in the chest before encircling his torso and pinning his arms to his sides.

"What are you doing?" Kevin began to struggle, but then his eyes went wide…and his head grew bigger.

For a brief, horrifying moment, Lizbeth thought Jaime was squeezing him so hard his head was about to pop. Then she realized Kevin's entire body, what she could see of it around the tentacle, was not only growing, it was changing color. When he was approximately double his normal size and his skin had taken on a silvery sheen, Jaime let go and sent, "*Who's next?*"

Chapter Thirty

Silverpit Crater, the North Sea

Zach had dug into dozens of open gun apertures, mangling the cannons inside with his horn. The aliens hadn't fired on him even though he'd presented an impossible-to-miss target. He'd vaguely wondered why but was having too much of a blast ripping their ship apart to dwell on it. Just when he began to think they weren't going to fight back at all, he felt a sting along one of his hind legs.

He skittered around to see that a large aperture had opened, and a wave of aliens was pouring out of it. They were bipedal, smaller and thinner than the average human, and fully covered in dark suits that probably protected them from earth's atmosphere as much as from enemy fire. Their weapons belched a smaller version of the arrowheads' fiery blue orbs. The energy substance stung like the dickens, but otherwise didn't seem to be doing much damage.

Only a few of the soldiers were shooting, but Zach backed away anyways, trying to stay out of range as they fanned out in front and to the side of him. He was nearing the edge of the mothership and had just lifted his elytra to fly off when a dull boom alerted him to an attack from the rear. Pain shot through his abdomen and the next thing he knew, he'd shifted back into human form, sprawling onto his belly. He wrapped his fingers around the shaft of a projectile sticking out of his side. It looked like a harpoon, and if he'd been normal size, it would have skewered him. Since he was a giant, it did little actual damage, but the excruciating pain it caused and his inability to hold a shift told him it was made of iron. As soon as he pulled it out another appeared in his shoulder.

He reached up to pull that one out, too, but the foot soldiers opened fire. The blue orbs that had been mostly deflected by his beetle armor were much more effective against sensitive human flesh. Zach writhed in agony, twitching and spasming uncontrollably. Through eyes slitted in pain, he looked up at the sky, spotting a lone black bird circling far above him.

Caw.

In his head, he heard Kevin, "*We're coming, bro!*"

He tried to shout, "No!" but his jaw was clenched tight.

"*Jaime shared his biometal with us,*" Lizbeth sent. "*We're bigger and stronger now!*"

He tried to respond, to warn them off, but the foot soldiers kept up a steady stream of fire and he could barely think past the pain. He knew even if he managed to remove the harpoon from his shoulder, they'd only shoot him with another, so shifting was out, but he still had his training. The energy from the blue orbs was disrupting the electrical impulses in his muscles, that much was clear. Relaxation and focus, a form of meditative biofeedback, had always been his go-to strategy when under the gun.

As he attempted to redirect his body's pain receptors, he listened in on the Welcoming Committee's conversation, glad to hear they seemed to know what was going on.

Hawthorne: "*The foot soldiers forced Zach into an area that he hadn't torn up yet in order to get him in range of the harpoon. We land in the zone he already disabled.*"

Caitlin: "*We can assume they haven't used the big guns because of Zach's and Jaime's electrical discharge, but that could change at any moment.*"

Kevin: "*What about the arrowheads?*"

Hawthorne: "*They can't risk shooting their own people, so for now, we'll be dealing with foot soldiers.*"

Caitlin: "*They fired their harpoon after Zach lifted his beetle shell to fly, which means they knew that species' vulnerabilities. Since it took them a while to respond to his attack, I think they had to research it. Each of us must choose an animal to shift into, but don't hold that shift for more than a few minutes. We don't want to give them time to figure out its weaknesses.*"

Lizbeth: "*And we should shift into something with an exoskeleton to protect us.*"

Zach felt a lessening of the attack and turned onto his side facing the enemy. Half of the foot soldiers had run to intercept the flock of huge birds about to land on the damaged mother ship. It was the break he'd been waiting for. He crossed his arms over his chest, tucked his chin and rolled towards the foot soldiers who were still shooting at him. At approximately a hundred times their size, he was a human – or Fae – steamroller.

Chapter Thirty-one

Silverpit Crater, the North Sea

As soon as Kevin landed on the dull, dark surface of the alien spaceship, he shifted into a crab, the only animal he could think of that was shielded, fast, and might do some damage. It was also the only animal whose anatomy he was entirely familiar with – he'd eaten enough stone crabs from the Texas gulf coast to fill a dumpster with his leavings.

To his left, he saw an armadillo and to his right, an ordinary-looking beetle. A group of foot soldiers opened fire, and the beetle turned itself around. For a moment, Kevin thought the beetle, whoever it was, was going to run away, but then, with a loud popping sound, it shot something repeatedly from the tip of its abdomen, spraying the nearest aliens with a steaming, foul-smelling liquid.

"*Ha HA!*" Tanie, the quiet one, gloated. "*How you like Bombardier Beetle juice, alien scum?!*"

He felt a series of mild stings as a few of the alien soldiers targeted him. As payback, he scuttled right for them, reaching out with his claws and pinching two of them as hard as he could. Their body armor cracked under the pressure and they both went limp. He tossed their bodies aside, feeling no remorse whatsoever.

Peripherally, he was aware of the others fighting alongside him. A rhinoceros, a crocodile or alligator, he couldn't tell which, a spider shooting sticky web at the enemy. The spider's exoskeleton didn't protect it as well as some of the other armored creatures' and it went down under a hail of fire. Kevin rushed the shooters and knocked them over, then flailed this way and that with his claws, mowing down a satisfying number.

91

He glanced over to where Zach had been and saw that he'd gotten the upper hand over the foot soldiers that had pinned him down earlier. Most of the soldiers were lying prone, and Zach was kneeling beside them. He swept his huge hand through their ranks, sending them flying off the side of the ship.

Kevin glanced back over to the spider, but it was no longer there. Another crab had taken its place and was pinching every soldier it could get its claws on.

Within a surprisingly short amount of time, the foot soldiers had been defeated, but within moments of the last alien falling, one of the other mother ships began to move.

"*Are they leaving?*" Lizbeth sent.

The mother ship rose and then moved to hover directly above them. As its shadow slid across the damaged surface of its companion ship, Kevin sent, "*I think we should get out of here.*"

Chapter Thirty-two

Silverpit Crater, the North Sea

Lizbeth agreed wholeheartedly with Kevin's assessment that they should beat a hasty retreat. Along with most of the others, she shifted back into a condor and began running for the edge to launch into flight, but it was too late. She heard an ominous *boom*-thwup-thwup-thwup, and glanced over her shoulder. Zach, the biggest of them and still in human form, rose to his full height and swatted at the net spinning towards her. With the distinctive sound of metal links clashing against each other, it wrapped around his hand, and he bellowed in pain, dropping to his knees with such force it shook the ship below her feet.

Lizbeth kept running. As much as she wanted to help him, his sacrifice would be in vain if she was caught. She heard it when more nets were deployed; heard the screams of her companions when the iron touched them.

She made it to the edge and hurled herself over, sick to her stomach and sick at heart. She kept her wings tucked tight to her sides, plummeting towards the sea. When she'd nearly reached the surface, she opened her wings just long enough to slow her descent before diving under. She shifted into the fastest sea creature she could think of – a mako shark – and swam straight down.

Caitlin had once told them that as air-breathers, they couldn't shift into fish. That was then, but now that Lizbeth's body mass was more than half biometal, she didn't have to breathe at all. She had no idea how or why that was, but she hoped her body would now also be able to handle the pressure of a deep-sea dive.

93

As she swam, she listened. One by one, her companions' panicked inner voices were silenced. She knew this could simply be a result of the iron netting preventing them from mind talk, but it frightened her nonetheless. She swam faster.

With her shark eyes, she saw the bottom of the ocean, but it was her Fae senses that led her to the very center of the impact crater. She nudged the sand with her snout, realizing as she did so that she had no idea why she'd come. Kevin had told them why he'd decided against putting the biometal in Jaime's body back into the grid. The aliens would benefit as much as the Fae, if not more. So what could she possibly hope to find in this place other than an end to her headlong flight, where grief could catch up with her?

If sharks could cry, she'd be bawling her eyes out. She wished she could destroy the biometal in her body so the aliens would never get hold of it. Not that that would stop them. They were going to kill her friends like they killed the Ir. Then they'd enslave all of mankind...

Lizbeth shook her head back and forth.

No.

She rammed her sensitive snout into the sand, screaming in her mind, *"No, no, no, no, no!"*

That didn't help matters, of course. Her fins stopped moving and she slowly settled on the sea floor as the silt she'd disturbed floated around her, clouding the formerly clear water.

In her anguish, her thoughts were fractured. She considered pulling more biometal from the earth and making herself even bigger than Zach, but she didn't know how. Kevin was the only one who'd been able to call the biometal. Why, she had no idea. Caitlin would say that each of them had their own strengths. Well, Lizbeth's pickpocketing skill wasn't going to help her now. Unless she could pull off a Hail Mary and steal control of the earth's magnetic field...

Her fins twitched. She couldn't make the biometal come to *her*, but maybe, just maybe she could go to *it*. But of all the creatures on earth, what could she become that would take her through minute cracks in solid rock to the depths of the lithosphere?

With a blinding flash of insight, she thought, *Not earth*. Not a creature from this planet, but one from so far away in space and time that they no longer existed. Except deep within her genome.

She was so certain she'd stumbled upon the answer that she didn't even have to ask herself how to do it. She just did.

Chapter Thirty-three

Silverpit Crater, the North Sea

Of them all, Zach was the last to get caught.

His evasive success hadn't been solely due to his size, although the others did fit neatly under the iron nets the aliens deployed. It was the memory of a comment Kevin had made, that the Ir could take unlimited shapes, which gave Zach an additional advantage over the others. Since Zach was technically more biometal than human, he figured he should be able to force his body into whatever shape he liked.

So that's what he did.

When he saw a harpoon that he wouldn't be able to dodge, he opened up a hole in his chest or leg or abdomen that let it pass straight through. Unfortunately for Zach, once the others were disabled, the aliens focused their attack on him again. The harpoons and nets came fast and furious and he couldn't see them all coming.

Once he was down, the aliens lashed him to the ship's exterior with iron cables, like some kind of futuristic Gulliver. He immediately began the relaxation and focus process that had enabled him to divert the worst of the pain and spasms the last time. Once he'd gotten it down to acceptable levels, he turned his head.

Kevin was trapped under a net not far from him.

"Kev," he said through teeth he couldn't seem to unclench. "Hang in there, bro."

There was no response; he hadn't expected one.

The alien foot soldiers moved aside, and for a moment he thought it had something to do with his words, but then he saw the newcomer.

This alien was slightly larger than the soldiers, also bipedal, but differently proportioned, with a bigger head and shorter legs. It, too, wore protective armor, but its face plate was transparent, allowing Zach to see its ugly, fly-eyed face.

It gestured, and the nearest soldiers removed Kevin's netting. Several others stood over him with weapons at the ready.

Kevin got unsteadily to his feet, shuddering, hate and fear in his eyes.

"*Kevin Guzman,*" the alien sent. "*We can still negotiate a peaceful surrender.*"

The words caused a blood-red rage to rise within Zach, with a corresponding loss of control over the pain. He shut his eyes and deliberately tuned the conversation out in order to regain focus. He concentrated on the one thing that was keeping him sane: Lizbeth, and the fact that she'd gotten away.

By now she would back on the Truman, and he hoped she wouldn't allow sentimentality to stop her from letting the aircraft carrier's commander know the Welcoming Committee had failed, and that they should send whatever forces the Cataclysm-wrecked world had left to its disposal against the aliens. Because none of them could believe anything the aliens–

"*Can anyone hear me?*"

He opened his eyes, averting his gaze from Kevin and the boss alien. "*Lizbeth! Where are you?*"

"*You wouldn't believe me if I told you.*"

"*Like anything could surprise me now.*"

"*What if I said I merged my body with the grid and was now stretched around the globe thinner than a piano wire?*"

Zach blinked a few times. "*Oh, uh, how...?*"

"*Not important. Where are you?*"

"*Strapped down. Out of commission. They caught all of us. The aliens want us to surrender.*"

"*Well, I have control of the gossamer sphere. Will that help?*"

Zach almost laughed but didn't want to call attention to himself. "*You're freaking amazing, you know that? I'm sure the sphere will help earth...somehow...but I don't see us – me and the rest of the Welcoming Committee – getting out of this alive.*"

"*Zach–*"

"*Listen, I've been wanting to tell you something, and I don't have time to sugar it up. I love you, okay?*"

"*Likewise, but I've been thinking–*"

"*Likewise? Seriously, that's all I get?*"

"*Remember a few seconds ago when you said you didn't have time to sugar it up? I love you, too. We'll talk about it later, k? I think I know how to get you out of there.*"

Zach was all business again. "*Tell me.*"

"*You know the shields we put around the nukes?*"

"*Yeah.*"

"*Put one around yourself, like a personal shield.*"

"*Can't. Got iron cables holding me down.*"

"*Then how are you talking to me?*"

"*You're doing that, not me. I've got just enough control of my body to keep the pain from driving me insane.*"

"*There's got to be a way for you to tap into the gossamer sphere.*"

"*You mean tap into you?*"

"*Har har.*"

"*Sorry, babe, like I said, we're all out of commis–*" he stopped and looked at Kevin, who directed a meaningful sidelong glance Zach's way before turning his attention back to the alien commander.

Chapter Thirty-four

Silverpit Crater, the North Sea

Kevin had been listening to the alien outline its exhaustive terms for surrender when Lizbeth made contact with Zach. He eavesdropped on his friends' conversation but didn't contribute for fear the alien might intercept it. Since he was the only one not currently bound by iron, he was the obvious person to test Lizbeth's personal shield theory, but for the moment, he felt more in need of a shield to protect his thoughts. Still, in a corner of his mind he couldn't stop himself from analyzing the theory's chances of success.

The shields he and the others had created to stop the nukes had been all-encompassing and isolating. Nothing could get in or out. The shield the aliens had formed around their mother ships had been flexible enough to allow birds to penetrate it. That shield was likely responsible for the instrument malfunction whenever a boat or plane strayed too close. He also suspected it was the real reason the aliens had maintained four days of silence – they *couldn't* communicate from behind their shield – and if they couldn't do it, neither could he.

Shielding himself might protect him from further harm, but it would also isolate him, and it would do nothing to help his friends.

The alien commander had been droning on, requiring little acknowledgment from Kevin, but it sounded like the commander was wrapping things up.

"*It's now or never, bro,*" Zach sent.

Something told Kevin this gambit wouldn't work, but he took a leap of faith and formed a shield around himself. The alien commander's words instantly ceased, and inside the transparent, spherical blue force field, Kevin sighed in relief. Outside, the aliens exploded into action.

Kevin watched without flinching as the foot soldiers fired at him repeatedly. The energy projectiles hit the shield with no effect, until the commander gestured for his soldiers to stop. As soon as the commander grabbed one of his solders' weapons and marched over to where Tara lay trapped under an iron net, Kevin realized his mistake. The commander lowered the muzzle to within inches of Tara's face and looked back at him.

Kevin hung his head, but only for as long as it took him to transcend his self-imposed limitations. With no warning of his intentions, he expanded the shield around him. It simultaneously encompassed his friends and pushed everything else away.

Chapter Thirty-five

Silverpit Crater, the North Sea

It took Lizbeth a while to get used to her new state of existence. After she spoke with Zach, she managed to completely disassociate from her very distracting physical self in order to merge her gossamers with earth's intangible forces. The result was an instantaneous influx of data that overwhelmed her. Her mind was forced to stretch beyond its limits to incorporate a dynamic map of all the electrical activity on the planet and in near space, all the way down to the smallest spark. If she hadn't reined the expansion in by focusing on one simple thing, she was sure it would have blown her mind out like a spent lightbulb filament.

That one thing was Zach.

When she'd spoken to him before, she'd been blind. She'd called out, "*Can anyone hear me*?" because she didn't have a clue where any of them were. Now she 'saw' them like never before; saw the dynamic, iridescent and luminescent currents pulsing through their bodies. It was magnificent, as if she'd glimpsed their very souls.

Lizbeth was with Kevin when he formed the shield around himself. It isolated him from everyone and everything – except her. She'd been about to speak to him when she sensed the alien commander's anger. When the commander threatened Tara, she knew from its aura that it wasn't bluffing.

But Kevin didn't give the commander a chance to prove its intentions.

From Lizbeth's perspective, Kevin's shield took on the properties of a supercharged soap bubble, allowing similar substances – the biometal energy coursing through and protectively enveloping Fae bodies – to pass through its membrane, while repelling everything else. It was the coup of a lifetime, but she didn't stop to congratulate him.

With zero fanfare, she pushed the alien mother ships out of earth's atmosphere on a direct course for the sun, uncaring that the aliens still standing on the exterior were killed. The mother ships fired their engines and stopped their progress, but just to show them how much control she had, she contacted them.

"*Attention alien scum. This is the people of earth. You are no longer welcome on our planet, in our solar system, or in our galaxy.*"

To illustrate her point, she shoved them towards the sun again, easily overpowering their engines. When they stopped themselves a second time, she sent a final message, "*Leave. Now. If you or any of your people ever come back, you will not live long enough to regret it.*"

Chapter Thirty-six

Flamborough, England

"So the next thing I know, I've come out of it to find myself buried under the others on the bottom of a giant floating bubble," Colonel Paxton said.

General Hawthorne laughed. "We were like a bunch of bloody fish flopping around in a net."

They were back on dry land in the mess tent. The tables and seating had been removed, but it was so crowded with British Army and American Navy personnel, local townsfolk, and dignitaries from several countries that people were spilling out onto the grounds of the tent city. Officers mingled with enlisted as everyone celebrated humanity's incredible victory.

Zach stayed glued to Lizbeth's side, touching her at every opportunity. She didn't seem to mind the PDA, but she was distracted, and he completely understood. She'd emerged from the depths of the earth physically intact, but out of necessity, mentally fractured. With her help, the Welcoming Committee had removed the bulk of the biometal from their bodies and replaced it in the lithosphere, repairing the grid so Lizbeth could be free of it. The protection of earth through a working gossamer sphere was of paramount importance, but the sphere was of no use to them without someone to control it, so Lizbeth had left a part of herself behind to do just that. She was now and forever bound to "the ethereal," as she referred to it.

Most of the Welcoming Committee were in attendance, standing at the back of the tent. The crowd was boisterous, but every time Lizbeth spoke, those nearby quieted down to hear her. She looked at Corporal Doyle, who had apparently gotten over his standoffishness to hang out with them. "Were you ever going to tell us?" she asked.

Doyle's face went ashen. After a moment, he mumbled, "Not if I didn't have to."

Caitlin, standing within the circle of Bill's possessive arm, narrowed her eyes at him. "Tell us what?"

Doyle stared at the ground. "I'm—I mean, I *was*—Guild."

Zach had figured there was something off about the guy from the moment he met him, but still, the admission shocked him. Zach's free hand clenched into a fist, but then he relaxed his fingers. Every one of them had changed profoundly. Doyle had fought beside him. No matter what his intentions were at the start, he was one of Zach's brothers now.

"You have to know you're forgiven," Lizbeth said.

Doyle looked up, eyes brimming with tears. "I know."

Caitlin took a deep breath and let it out slowly. "The old ways are gone."

"The old ways," Seamus said, "were based in superstition and ignorance."

General Hawthorne offered Doyle a tight-lipped smile. "Intel on who you were working with will go a long way towards salvaging your career, Corporal."

"Yes, sir."

Doyle's discomfiture was almost painful for Zach to watch, so he glanced away. Over Lizbeth's shoulder, he saw Mr. Winters and his wife Bess. He turned to catch Jaime's eye and jerked his head towards them. Jaime smiled broadly and lifted an arm to wave them over.

After introducing them all around, Jaime began telling the story of how they got the chicken. He had a flair for the dramatic, turning a simple tale into an epic adventure. Mr. Winters interjected several times, but his wife kept silent, a melancholy look in her eyes. When the story was finished and someone else had taken the stage, Lizbeth took Bess Winters' hand, and held the other one out to Mr. Winters. He put his rough, blunt-fingered hand into hers with an inquiring look.

"Tell me about your daughter," she said.

Bess tried to take her hand away, but Mr. Winters said, "She was every star in the evenin' sky."

Lizbeth's silvery eyes were intense. "You said she was in New Zealand during the Cataclysm, right?"

"Yes."

"Confirmed dead?"

Bess yanked her hand away, putting her knuckles to her lips. Mr. Winters scowled down at Lizbeth. "Not confirmed. Communication with the survivor camps has been near impossible. The government's gone, there are no cell towers, only a few intact land lines, and most of the humanitarian aid ships have been hijacked by pirates. We've sent inquiries but have never gotten a reply. Why do you ask?"

Lizbeth held her hand out to Bess again. "Let me feel her."

"What?" Bess whispered.

Zach, realizing what Lizbeth wanted to attempt, but not wanting to raise the Winters' hopes, said, "Please."

Mr. Winters put his arm around his wife, his free hand still clasped by Lizbeth. "What do you want us to do?"

"Just think of her," Lizbeth said.

In his head, Zach heard Kevin say, "*Let's help her out.*"

The mess tent began to quiet as every Fae inside abandoned whatever they'd been doing or saying to gather around the grieving couple.

Zach closed his eyes to savor the sensation of his gossamers melding with Lizbeth's, an exquisite dichotomy of pinpoint focus and diffuse expansion. In his mind, he saw the earth from her perspective – or rather, from the sphere's perspective – like being at the center of a spun glass fiber optic chandelier. Lizbeth had complete control over it, and he and the other Fae went along for the ride as they zipped across land and ocean, traveling to what was left of the New Zealand islands. Lizbeth sorted through the multitude of energy signatures, eliminating all but those produced by the human body. She then touched upon each of those, so rapidly Zach had to fight against dizziness as auras flew past like freeway lights photographed with the shutter speed wide open.

Suddenly they stopped and Zach heard Bess cry out, "Emily!"

He opened his eyes and saw what appeared to be a bluish hologram of a young woman standing before him. Her painfully thin arms were crossed over her chest, sunken eyes downturned.

"Can she see us?" Mr. Winters asked.

Lizbeth shook her head. "No, but…hold on."

The hologram winked out of existence, eliciting a sob from Bess. Zach was still connected to Lizbeth and couldn't hold back a grin of anticipation.

The other Fae began to walk through the crowd, asking people to step back until a path to the tent flap was cleared.

He knew from personal experience that the wait wouldn't be long. After he and the others were rescued from the aliens by Kevin's shield, Lizbeth had transported them almost instantly to the Truman through the same method the aliens used to travel through interstellar space. Emily Winters was the breadth of a world away, but she was about to find out that the rules of physics meant nothing to the gossamer sphere.

Chapter Thirty-seven

Flamborough, England

Kevin linked his fingers with Tara's and watched as avidly as anyone present when the orb shield carrying Emily Winters arrived. It entered the tent and floated up the cleared aisle before dissipating. A filthy, red-haired young woman knelt before the assemblage, her eyes wide and frightened until she saw her parents. Then she jumped to her feet and threw herself into their arms.

The reunion was beyond poignant. Tears fell and explanations were breathlessly offered. After Emily ate the first real meal she'd had in months, her parents took her off to get cleaned up and examined by the local doctor.

Kevin stood in a corner of the tent with Tara, silently observing. It was the first time since the Cataclysm began that he felt truly contented. The aliens were gone, headed on a course that would take them out of the solar system, but since they no longer had access to earth's sphere, they were unable to use their interstellar engines. They were, as one of the RAF pilots in attendance put it, "A dead stick." It comforted Kevin to know they wouldn't be able to call for help, either. They were in for a very long journey to the nearest system with a sphere they could use, which according to Lizbeth was not within the Milky Way.

He spotted Lizbeth by the punch bowl. She'd changed drastically from the girl he'd met almost a year ago. That girl had been resentful because she wouldn't be able to afford college, and reluctant to enter into a new adventure. Now she was fearless and ferociously determined to protect the denizens of earth, even if it meant giving away a part of herself.

Zach had been in orbit around her since she'd returned. He'd changed, too. Matured, although Kevin would never admit that aloud. Zach would always be somewhat brash and irreverent, but the biting criticism he'd often directed Kevin's way had vanished. Where before Kevin might have said he and Zach would never see eye to eye, now he knew they would be lifelong friends.

He looked around for Tainie and found her standing between Caitlin and Seamus. It still felt weird to think of her as his sister. They'd never gotten a chance to really talk, but his earlier reticence on that score had disappeared. They had a lot to catch up on and he was looking forward to it.

Caitlin turned and smiled at him. *"Penny for your thoughts."*

"Just thinking how much we've all changed."

Next to her, Seamus lifted his plastic cup. "I'd like to propose a toast."

A good-natured groan rose from the crowd.

"I promise to keep it relatively short." Seamus chuckled. "Especially since I doubt I'll be able to adequately put into words what is in my heart."

There were nods and murmurs of assent all around.

"But I know someone who can," Seamus said with a mischievous grin. He shifted into H. Q. Spencer, and the crowd laughed.

Seamus waited for them to quiet down before continuing. "Nine months ago, like all the rest of my brethren, I was in hiding. All the world thought the Fae were fairy-tale creatures invented by some fertile mind a thousand years ago. Well, almost all. There were others who knew we were real, and who considered us a threat that needed exterminating.

"Not to sound like I'm tooting my own horn, but had they succeeded, none of us would be standing here today."

He held a hand out to indicate Caitlin. "Here stands the one who should be tooting."

Caitlin rolled her eyes as everyone laughed again.

"She's genuine royalty," Seamus said, "The granddaughter of one of the first three shapeshifters to ever exist on this planet. The last Noble. When the anomalies related to the gossamer sphere's attempt to tune itself first began, Caitlin alone knew what it meant."

"Suspected," Caitlin said.

"A suspicion strong enough to come out of hiding in order to recruit the help of three young heroes – Kevin, Lizbeth, and Zach."

Kevin felt his cheeks go hot. He glanced down at Tara, who slipped her arm around his waist and looked up at him adoringly.

"And along the way, our numbers grew. Tainie, Tara, Jaime, Bill, Hawthorne, Paxton, and Doyle, just to name the…names I remember off the top of my head."

Another laugh.

"But I'm not offering a toast to the Fae tonight," Seamus said. "No, tonight we're toasting those we lost since the Cataclysm first began changing our world." He raised his glass higher.

"To our friends and family who were taken too soon. May they smile down upon our victory!"

The end.

www.ingramcontent.com/pod-product-compliance
Lightning Source LLC
Chambersburg PA
CBHW070634130626
46555CB00006B/2543